OPERATION DIPLOMAT

DIPLOMAT

Francis Durbridge

WILLIAMS & WHITING

Cover design by Timo Schroeder

9781915887160

Williams & Whiting (Publishers)

15 Chestnut Grove, Hurstpierpoint,

West Sussex, BN6 9SS

Titles by Francis Durbridge published by Williams & Whiting

1 The Scarf – tv serial
2 Paul Temple and the Curzon Case – radio serial
3 La Boutique – radio serial
4 The Broken Horseshoe – tv serial
5 Three Plays for Radio Volume 1
6 Send for Paul Temple – radio serial
7 A Time of Day – tv serial
8 Death Comes to The Hibiscus – stage play
  The Essential Heart – radio play
  (writing as Nicholas Vane)
9 Send for Paul Temple – stage play
10 The Teckman Biography – tv serial
11 Paul Temple and Steve – radio serial
12 Twenty Minutes From Rome – a teleplay
13 Portrait of Alison – tv serial
14 Paul Temple: Two Plays for Radio Volume 1
15 Three Plays for Radio Volume 2
16 The Other Man – tv serial
17 Paul Temple and the Spencer Affair – radio serial
18 Step In The Dark – film script
19 My Friend Charles – tv serial
20 A Case For Paul Temple – radio serial
21 Murder In The Media – more rediscovered serials and
   stories
22 The Desperate People – tv serial
23 Paul Temple: Two Plays for Television
24 And Anthony Sherwood Laughed – radio series
25 The World of Tim Frazer – tv serial
26 Paul Temple Intervenes – radio serial
27 Passport To Danger! – radio serial
28 Bat Out of Hell – tv serial
29 Send For Paul Temple Again – radio serial
30 Mr Hartington Died Tomorrow – radio serial

Murder At The Weekend – the rediscovered newspaper serials and short stories

Also published by Williams & Whiting:
Francis Durbridge : The Complete Guide
By Melvyn Barnes

Titles by Francis Durbridge to be published by Williams & Whiting

Murder On The Continent (Further re-discovered serials and stories)

Paul Temple and the Alex Affair

Paul Temple and the Canterbury Case (film script)

Paul Temple and the Conrad Case

Paul Temple and the Geneva Mystery

Paul Temple and the Margo Mystery

Paul Temple: Two Plays For Radio Vol 2 (Send For Paul Temple and News of Paul Temple)

The Passenger

INTRODUCTION

Francis Durbridge (1912-98) is not only remembered as the creator of the radio detective Paul Temple, but as a television dramatist who kept viewers guessing from 1952 to 1980 and the writer of nine intriguing stage plays including *Suddenly at Home, Murder with Love* and *House Guest.*

His television career began impressively, when *The Broken Horseshoe* (15 March to 19 April 1952) became the first thriller serial on British television – defined as a plot continuing over several episodes rather than a series of individual complete stories. Indeed it prompted C.A. Lejeune to review it in her *Observer* column (23 March 1952) in terms that now seem extraordinary. She wrote: "It will be interesting to see how Mr. Durbridge manages his 're-capping' from week to week, for *The Broken Horseshoe* is a true serial and not a series of associated adventures with a beginning, middle and end. The skill with which such a programme can arrange for new viewers to start viewing here, without boring old viewers or wasting time, will achieve much to do with the serial's success. But if it goes on as well as it has begun, I don't intend to miss a Saturday." From this it appears that Lejeune saw Durbridge as an innovator, although he had been doing that very thing for nearly fifteen years with his Paul Temple serials on the radio!

Operation Diplomat was televised by the BBC as a swift follow-up to *The Broken Horseshoe*, in six thirty-minute episodes from 25 October to 29 November 1952. Like its predecessor it was produced and directed by Martyn C. Webster, who had been Durbridge's radio producer since the 1930s – and when they turned to television the duo continued to justify their longstanding radio reputation for stunning cliff-hanger endings to every episode. Incidentally, it's noteworthy that in *Operation Diplomat* the part of

Edward Schroder was played by Peter Coke, who assumed the mantle of Paul Temple on BBC radio very soon afterwards and was to become the definitive voice in this role.

While it might have been Durbridge's original intention to create a television series, just as he had done with Paul Temple on the radio, it would surely have been unrealistic for hospital surgeon Mark Fenton (played by John Robinson in *The Broken Horseshoe* and Hector Ross in *Operation Diplomat*) to become accidentally involved in murder cases time and time again. So from that point Durbridge wrote one-off television serials, and continued to do so for nearly thirty years. They attracted a huge body of fans in the UK and internationally, with audiences gripped by thrillers such as *Portrait of Alison, My Friend Charles, The Other Man, The Scarf, The World of Tim Frazer, Melissa* and *Bat Out of Hell*. And it is worth noting that Durbridge always remained loyal to the BBC, in spite of blandishments from the new commercial television channel ITV.

At this point, however, it might be helpful to put Durbridge in context, because by the time he turned to television he had for twenty years been a prolific writer of sketches, stories, plays and serials for BBC radio. He had begun with children's stories and light comedies, including libretti for musical plays, but a talent for crime fiction became evident in his early radio plays *Murder in the Midlands* (1934) and *Murder in the Embassy* (1937). The *Radio Times* (11 February 1938) mentioned that he had by then written some one hundred radio pieces, and Charles Hatton commented in *Radio Pictorial* (28 October 1938) that "He is one of the very few people in this country who have succeeded in making a living by writing for the BBC."

Durbridge continued to write plays and serials for BBC radio for many years, using his own name and occasionally the pseudonyms Frank Cromwell, Nicholas Vane and Lewis Middleton Harvey, while capitalising on the particular brainwave that ensured his longstanding reputation. In 1938 he hit on the dream team of novelist/detective Paul Temple and his wife Steve, with the audience reaction to his radio serial *Send for Paul Temple* leading to sequels over several decades that built an impressive UK and European fanbase. In response to his fan mail following *Send for Paul Temple* in 1938, which attracted over 7,000 letters to the BBC asking for more, he immediately followed up later the same year with *Paul Temple and the Front Page Men*. Then from 1939 to 1968 there were another twenty-six Paul Temple cases, of which seven were new productions of earlier broadcasts.

Having become arguably the pre-eminent writer of mystery thrillers for radio, it was natural that Durbridge should join the rush of writers into television. Indeed this was much later confirmed in a published interview (*Radio Times*, 21 October 1971) when he said: "Twenty years ago in the United States, a producer told me that I was wasting my time by not going into television. So that's what I did – I tried to build up a reputation with serials, since I'd vowed never to write a Paul Temple episode for television."

But Durbridge became a multi-media playwright, and it was not surprising that *Operation Diplomat*, like its television predecessor *The Broken Horseshoe*, was soon turned into a cinema film because four movies based on Durbridge's Paul Temple radio serials had already proved popular. The 1953 Butchers/Nettlefold production *Operation Diplomat* credited the screenplay to A.R. Rawlinson and John Guillermin, with Guillermin also directing and Ernest G. Ray the producer. As the film industry at that time tended to cast popular actors from the cinema world in the leading roles rather than actors from television, Hector Ross was replaced by movie favourite Guy Rolfe as Mark Fenton. A DVD of the film was marketed by Renown Pictures in 2011, but the original television production was never repeated or novelised.

So do enjoy this script, which reflects Francis Durbridge's earliest days on the small screen.

Melvyn Barnes
Author of *Francis Durbridge: The Complete Guide* (Williams & Whiting, 2018)

This book reproduces Francis Durbridge's original script together with the list of characters and actors of the BBC programme on the dates mentioned, but the eventual broadcast might have edited Durbridge's script in respect of scenes, dialogue and character names.

OPERATION DIPLOMAT

A serial in six episodes

By FRANCIS DURBRIDGE

Broadcast on BBC Television

25th October – 29th November1952

CAST:

Mark Fenton . . . . Hector Ross

Edward Schroder . . . . .Peter Coke

Det Insp Austin . . . . Raymond Huntley

CID Photographer . . . . James Beattie

Det Sgt Lewis . . . . .Alun Owen

Colonel Wyman . . . . .Ivan Samson

Sister Rogers . . . . Elizabeth Maude

Mrs Terry . . . . .Lilian Christine

Robin Terry . . . . .David Peel

Nurse . . . . Nancy Manningham

Wade . . . . Reginald Hearne

Morgan . . . . .Duncan McIntyre

Linda Brooks . . . . Pamela Galloway

Sir Oliver Peters . . . . .Arthur Ridley

Dr Andrew Sefton . . . . .Hugh Kelly

Oscar . . . . Raf de la Torre

Mrs Dobson . . . . .Fanny Carby

Harrison . . . . Roger Delgado

Police Sergeant . . . . .Stanley Groome

Det Insp Lester . . . . .Cecil Winter

Michael Christie . . . . .Brian Badcoe

Collins . . . . .Charles Leno

Det Sgt Compton . . . . . Christopher Rhodes

Mrs Christie . . . . Mary Horn

Other parts played by Venetia Barrett,
Kathleen Canty, James Beattie, Arthur Mason,
Nikola Sterne, Frank Singuineau,
Ann Totten and Dorit Welles

EPISODE ONE

SIR OLIVER PETERS

OPEN TO: The Drawing Room of Mark Fenton's Flat. Evening.

The body of EDWARD SCHRODER is on the carpeted floor in front of the window. A pane of glass is broken., having been shattered by the bullet which killed Schroder. There is a carton of "Mercury" (American) cigarettes by the side of the body.

MARK FENTON is sitting in an armchair. He looks on edge.

DET INSP AUSTIN is examining the body.

WILSON, a CID photographer takes several flashlight photographs of the dead man.

AUSTIN: All right, Wilson.

When the photographs have been taken the INSPECTOR nods to WILSON, who, after a casual glance at FENTON, goes out.

AUSTIN moves to FENTON and indicates the body.

AUSTIN: You say his name's Schroder?

FENTON: Yes. Edward Schroder.

AUSTIN: Is he a friend of yours?

FENTON: No, I've told you – he's not a friend of mine.

AUSTIN: (*Officiously*) Then what's he doing here? Why did he come to see you?

FENTON rises.

FENTON: Because he wanted to explain about … Look, Inspector, it's no good asking me these questions. I refuse to say anything until I've seen Colonel Wyman.

AUSTIN: You mentioned this fellow Wyman before! Who is he? Is he your lawyer?

FENTON: No, he's one of your people. He's attached to the Special Branch.

AUSTIN: But this isn't anything to do with the Special Branch! It's a plain case of murder. Now look,

3

	Mr Fenton, sooner or later you've got to make a statement and when you do …
FENTON:	I shall make it to Colonel Wyman – no one else.
AUSTIN:	(*Deciding not to lose his temper*) All right, Mr Fenton, if that's the way you want it. We've met before, haven't we, sir?
FENTON:	I don't remember.
AUSTIN:	(*Nodding*) George Bellamy, your brother-in-law, introduced us just before he left Scotland Yard and went out to South Africa.
FENTON:	Oh, yes.
AUSTIN:	Mr Fenton, has this business got anything to do with The Broken Horseshoe?
FENTON:	No, nothing. Nothing at all.
AUSTIN:	Well, what happened?
FENTON:	I've told you, I'm not …
AUSTIN:	(*Interrupting FENTON*) All right – all right – I don't want the whole story. I only want to know what happened to Schroder, that's all. Did you murder him?
FENTON:	No, of course I didn't!
AUSTIN:	Why, of course? It's your flat. The constable heard the shot – he found the body here.
FENTON:	If the constable heard the shot then he must know perfectly well that it was fired from across the street. Schroder was standing in front of the window; we were talking. I went out to get Schroder a drink and …

DET SGT LEWIS enters.

AUSTIN:	Yes, what is it, sergeant?
LEWIS:	There's a Colonel Wyman called, sir – he says he's got an appointment with Mr Fenton.
AUSTIN:	Yes, all right. Show him is.

4

LEWIS: Yes, sir.

LEWIS turns and opens a door.

LEWIS: Come in, sir.

COLONEL WYMAN enters. He is a rather serious looking man in his early fifties. He wears glasses and has a faintly aloof – almost disconcerting – manner.

AUSTIN: Colonel Wyman?

WYMAN: Yes.

FENTON: Colonel, I've got to talk to you privately. The reason I phoned …

AUSTIN: One moment, Mr Fenton. I'm Detective-Inspector Austin, sir. I understand that Mr Fenton here telephoned you shortly after this man – Edward Schroder – was murdered.

WYMAN looks down at SCHRODER, then across at FENTON.

There is a slight pause.

WYMAN: Mr Fenton telephoned me – yes.

AUSTIN: (*Irritatedly*) Well, for reasons best known to himself, he refused to make a statement until he could talk to you, sir. Now I don't know how you fit into the picture, Colonel, but …

WYMAN: I don't. I've never seen this man before and I've only met Mr Fenton once; that was three weeks ago when we played golf together.

WYMAN looks down at SCHRODER's body again.

WYMAN: When was this man … What did you say his name was?

AUSTIN: Edward Schroder.

WYMAN: When was he murdered?

AUSTIN: About fifteen minutes ago.

WYMAN: I see.

WYMAN looks at FENTON.

WYMAN: Well, my appointment with Mr Fenton was made at eleven o'clock this morning. He telephoned me from St Mathew's Hospital and asked me to meet him here at six o'clock.

WYMAN takes his watch from his waistcoat.

WYMAN: It's now …

WYMAN peers at his watch.

WYMAN: …precisely four minutes past.

AUSTIN: (*To FENTON; surprised*) Is this true?

FENTON: Yes.

AUSTIN: (*Puzzled*) Then you actually telephoned Colonel Wyman this morning – at eleven o'clock – before the murder took place?

FENTON: Yes.

AUSTIN: Did you know that Schroder was going to be murdered?

FENTON: No, of course I didn't!

AUSTIN: Then why did you send for Colonel Wyman?

There is a slight pause.

FENTON hesitates.

WYMAN: (*To FENTON*) When you telephoned me you said the matter was urgent. If I remember rightly you used the phrase 'desperately urgent'.

FENTON: I did.

WYMAN: (*With a faint note of sarcasm*) Well, anything you've got to say to me, Mr Fenton – however 'desperately urgent' – can be said in front of Inspector Austin.

FENTON looks worried; uncertain of himself.

FENTON: (*With almost a sigh of relief*) All right, if that's the way you want it. God knows, I've got to tell somebody about this! I've got to tell this story in my own way. I've got to start

6

at the beginning – the very beginning – otherwise you just won't believe me.

WYMAN: Let's sit down.

They all sit down.

WYMAN: Go on …

FENTON: It started four days ago at St Mathew's Hospital. (*Thoughtfully*) Four days ago … the afternoon of Tuesday, October the 21st. I was examining a patient called Mrs Terry …

CUT TO: A Corridor of St Mathew's Hospital. Day.

Nurse, doctors, etc are walking up and down the corridor.
SISTER ROGERS passes down the corridor carrying a small tray bearing two cups of tea and a plate of biscuits, under her arm she carries copies of the evening papers. She enters FENTON's office.

CUT TO: FENTON's Office at St Mathew's Hospital. Day.

MRS TERRY is on a settee being examined by FENTON.
As he finishes his examination SISTER ROGERS enters and closes the door.

FENTON's voice heard over the action: …Mrs Terry was a widow; she was rather neurotic but she had great charm and a likeable personality. She was a private patient at the hospital and at the beginning of September I'd operated on her. Her progress had been impaired by certain minor complications.

FENTON moves away from the settee; he stands looking down at MRS TERRY.
MRS TERRY fastens her dressing gown. She looks up at FENTON; anxious for his decision.

MRS TERRY: Well, Mr Fenton?

7

FENTON: (*Smiling*) We don't want to lose you, Mrs
              Terry – but we think you ought to go.

MRS TERRY looks highly delighted.

MRS TERRY: Then I'm better?

FENTON: Well, I wouldn't say you were better.
              You're certainly a great deal better than you
              were. I want you to continue the …
              treatment and try and get just a little more
              exercise.

MRS TERRY: (*Very happy*) When can I leave, Mr Fenton?
              This morning?

FENTON: My word, we are popular, aren't we, Sister?
              You can leave tomorrow, Mrs Terry – if all
              goes well.

MRS TERRY: Tomorrow! Only twenty-four hours!

SISTER: (*Laughing*) It's a pity you can't get
              remission for good conduct!

MRS TERRY: I doubt whether I've earned it. I'm sure
              Sister Rogers doesn't think so. (*Laughing*)
              All those notes of mine flying backwards
              and forwards.

SISTER ROGERS laughs at MRS TERRY.

SISTER: Tea?

MRS TERRY: Thank you.

*SISTER ROGERS gives MRS TERRY a cup, and one to
FENTON. She then goes back to the table.*

There is a knock on the door.

FENTON: Come in.

*ROBIN TERRY pops his head round the door. He is a neat,
yet rather artistic young man. He carries a small oil
painting.*

FENTON: Oh! Come in, Mr Terry!

MRS TERRY: Hello, Robin!

ROBIN: Hello, mother! I popped upstairs but they
              told me you were with Mr Fenton.
MRS TERRY: I've got a surprise for you, Robin. I'm
              coming home tomorrow.
ROBIN: (*To FENTON*) Is she really?
FENTON: (*Nodding*) Providing she takes things easy.
ROBIN: I say, that's jolly good news! Jolly good.

ROBIN indicates the painting.

ROBIN: Well, you won't be wanting this, Mardie. I
              thought it might brighten that little room of
              yours.

ROBIN props the painting up on the seat of a nearby chair.

ROBIN: I finished it last night. Bentick likes it, he's
              offered me fifty guineas for it.
MRS TERRY: (*Disappointed*) Oh, dear!
ROBIN: Don't you like it?
MRS TERRY: No, I don't! And you know perfectly well I
              wouldn't like it. Robin, why don't you paint
              like you used to? This isn't a bit pretty.
ROBIN: (*Amused*) It's not supposed to be pretty. If it
              was pretty Bentick wouldn't offer me fifty
              guineas for it.

ROBIN turns to FENTON who is staring at the picture.

ROBIN: Do you like it, Mr Fenton?
FENTON: Well – it's – certainly different.
ROBIN: (*Amused; to SISTER ROGERS*) Sister?
SISTER: (*Bluntly*) What's it supposed to be?
ROBIN: Ah! (*Laughing*) It's not supposed to be
              anything! It's abstract.
FENTON: Well, I'm afraid I like a tree to look like a
              tree!
SISTER: So do I.
MRS TERRY: I couldn't agree more.

ROBIN removes the painting from the chair.

9

ROBIN: Sold to Mr Bentick for fifty guineas!

They all laugh.

SISTER ROGERS picks up a cup.

FENTON goes to the table and glances casually at the front page of an evening newspaper.

SISTER: Would you like a cup of tea, Mr Terry?

ROBIN: No. Thank you, Sister.

FENTON: (*Surprised*) Good Lord.

SISTER: (*Turning*) What is it, Mr Fenton?

FENTON: (*Indicating the newspaper*) Have you seen this? Sir Oliver Peters has disappeared. They say he's in Moscow.

MRS TERRY: Sir Oliver Peters?

ROBIN: Yes, it was on the one o'clock news. There's all sorts of rumours – apparently he disappeared four days ago.

FENTON: But I can't believe it! Peters isn't a communist …

ROBIN: Well, whether he's a communist or not old boy, he's in Moscow.

SISTER ROGERS picks up the newspaper and looks at it.

FENTON: Yes, but I know Peters. I operated on him two years ago. He's the last person on earth you'd imagine to be a communist.

SISTER: There's something in the Stop Press. (*Reading*) "Unconfirmed reports from Belgrade say that Sir Oliver Peters, the missing British diplomat, arrived in Moscow on Thursday afternoon. He is reported to have looked extremely well and was carrying several books and a briefcase".

FENTON: I just don't believe it!

SISTER: (*Looking at the newspaper*) There's something else …

ROBIN: (*Reading over SISTER ROGERS' shoulder*) "Helsinki, Monday. A spokesman for the British Embassy is reported to have said that they have no knowledge of the whereabouts of Sir Oliver Peters ..." No knowledge! They know where he is all right! He's in Moscow!

MRS TERRY: Who is this Sir Oliver Peters, anyway?

FENTON: He's Chairman of the United Defence Committee. What he doesn't know about Western defence is nobody's business.

ROBIN: If you ask me, this is pretty serious.

FENTON: Yes.

SISTER: It's amazing, isn't it? Peters must have had everything he wanted in the world. Wealth ... position ... power.

The phone rings.

FENTON lifts the receiver.

FENTON: Hello? ... Yes, yes. I'll be up in about five minutes.

FENTON replaces the receiver.

He looks at his watch.

FENTON: Mrs Terry, I shan't be on duty tomorrow so don't forget what I told you. Take it easy for the first two or three weeks and then plenty of exercise.

MRS TERRY nods and takes a pencil and small writing pad out from her handbag.

MRS TERRY: I shan't forget, Mr Fenton. I'll make a note of it.

SISTER ROGERS laughs.

CUT TO: The Main Entrance of St Mathew's Hospital. Late Afternoon.

FENTON comes out of the hospital, hesitates on the steps and then looks up at the sky.

He walks down the steps.

CUT TO: *Fenton buying an evening newspaper at a newsstand. The newspaper placards on show say "PETERS IN MOSCOW?" – "MYSTERY OF MISSING DIPLOMAT" – "MISSING DIPLOMAT: CABINET CALLED".*

CUT TO: *FENTON slowly walking along, reading his paper.*

FENTON's voice over the action: When I reached Cranley Street, which is just off the Harrington Road, an ambulance drew into the kerb and a Nurse jumped out. It was obvious that an emergency had arisen.

An ambulance approaches from the background.

The ambulance draws into the kerb, quite near to FENTON, and the doors at the rear are thrown open.

Obviously intrigued, FENTON stops and turns towards the vehicle.

A NURSE jumps out of the ambulance.

NURSE: Mr Fenton?

FENTON: Yes?

NURSE: I hope you don't mind my asking the driver to stop, Mr Fenton. I could see you through the window. There is a man inside who is severely shocked, sir. Would you please have a look at him? I think he may have had a stroke.

FENTON takes the NURSE's arm.

FENTON: Yes, all right, nurse! Jump in!

CUT TO: Inside The Ambulance.

FENTON enters the ambulance, followed by the NURSE.

WADE is sitting inside the ambulance, near the single window, waiting for FENTON. WADE is in his late thirties, tough and poker-faced. He speaks with a slight Irish accent, and is very well dressed. His right hand is in his overcoat pocket.

The NURSE closes the door behind her and sits on the side seat facing WADE.

FENTON stares at WADE, puzzled.

FENTON: (*Turning to the NURSE*) What is this?

The NURSE doesn't reply.

WADE rises and leans forward and speaks to the driver of the ambulance.

The ambulance gathers speed.

FENTON: (*To the NURSE*) Who are you?

WADE: Relax, Mr Fenton! Take it easy.

WADE takes his hand from his pocket; he is holding a revolver.

WADE: My name is Wade. I'm sorry we had to pick you up this way.

FENTON: What is this? What's the idea?

WADE: Sit down, Mr Fenton. This is rather a confined space. If you start getting difficult it means I shall have to use this … (*He indicates the revolver*)

FENTON turns towards the door; the NURSE takes him by the arm restraining him.

FENTON: (*Raising his voice*) Stop this ambulance! Stop it! If you don't …

WADE sticks the revolver into FENTON's ribs: he obviously means business.

WADE: Sit down! (*Quietly: determined*) Sit down, Mr Fenton.

A moment.

FENTON sits.

WADE leans forward towards him.

WADE: Now let's get one thing straight. (*He indicates the revolver*) This isn't a toy. I don't want to use it and I shan't use it, not if you do what I tell you. But if you raise your voice again, or if there's any funny business, I shall pull this trigger as sure as God made little apples. Now don't let's have any illusions about that, there's a good fellow.

FENTON sits back: he watches WADE.

There is a slight pause.

FENTON: Where are you taking me?

WADE: We're taking you out of Town. Now relax. Relax … take it easy, Mr Fenton. That's right.

The NURSE puts a cushion behind FENTON's back.

He turns and looks at her, she meets his gaze.

WADE takes a cigarette case out of his pocket with his free hand and flicks it open.

The NURSE leans forward and takes a cigarette out of the case and puts it in WADE's mouth.

WADE offers FENTON a cigarette but FENTON shakes his head.

WADE replaces the case, takes out his lighter, flicks it and lights his cigarette.

There is a pause.

WADE: Do you mind if I ask you a personal question?

FENTON doesn't reply.

WADE: How much do you make a year?

FENTON doesn't reply.

WADE: (*Grinning*) It's o.k. I'm just curious. I'm not the Inland Revenue. (*He looks down at FENTON's hands*) You know, it's a funny thing. When I

14

was a kid I always wanted to be a surgeon. My old man was keen on it – he was dead keen. Then one day somebody told him I just hadn't got the right sort of hands for it.

WADE looks at his hands and across at FENTON's.

WADE: Let's have a look at your hands, Mr Fenton. Hold them out …

FENTON hesitates: then holds his hands out towards WADE.

WADE: Very nice. Very nice, to be sure. Aren't they, nurse?

The NURSE leans forward and suddenly clamps handcuffs on FENTON's wrist.

FENTON makes a movement but WADE leans forward with the revolver.

The NURSE clamps the second handcuff on FENTON's left wrist.

FENTON looks annoyed, then sinks back onto the seat.

FENTON: You're not taking any chances, are you, Mr Wade?

WADE: (*With the suggestion of a smile; pleased with himself*) No. (*He looks at the revolver again*) I think we can dispense with this now, don't you? Just between me and you, these things always make me just a little self-conscious.

WADE puts the revolver back into his pocket.

WADE: By the way, I'm afraid I shall have to blindfold you. Oh, not yet! Not for a long time. Towards the end of the journey. I think it's an unnecessary precaution, but those are my instructions.

FENTON: Where are you taking me to?

WADE: I told you, we're taking you out of Town. It's quite a journey so be sensible, my dear fellow,

15

and relax. (*Smiling*) You've nothing to worry about. Nothing at all …

CUT TO: *The Ambulance driving very fast out of Town.*

CUT TO: Inside the Ambulance.
The ambulance slows down during this short scene.
WADE is still sitting opposite FENTON, hand in his overcoat pocket, eyes half closed, watching.
During the following speech FENTON looks at his watch.
FENTON's voice: I don't know how long the journey lasted. I seemed to be in that ambulance for ages. I looked at my watch once and found that it had stopped at half-past eight. I figured that it must have been about a quarter past six when they picked me up. After a time the nurse produced a scarf and proceeded to blindfold me. I realised then that we were nearing our destination.

WADE glances behind the blind, and decides that they have finally reached their destination.
The NURSE also begins to move; looking slightly relieved. She takes a silk scarf from her pocket and proceeds to blindfold FENTON with it.
FENTON's voice: The ambulance slowed down; it seemed to me that we were entering the private drive of a large house.

The ambulance slows down, gradually to a standstill.
WADE rises; stretching himself.
He takes hold of FENTON's arm.
WADE: (*To the NURSE*) O.K., nurse – you go first.
The NURSE opens the door of the ambulance: a beam of light shines across the entrance.
WADE: Now watch the steps, Mr Fenton.

16

FENTON moves towards the exit at the back of the ambulance.

CUT TO: The Drawing Room of a large country house.
The room has been converted into a temporary operating theatre.

FENTON's voice: It wasn't until I was inside the house that they removed the handcuffs and untied the scarf.

We see EDWARD SCHRODER is in the room. He is wearing a white collar-high surgeon's jacket.

FENTON's voice: It was then that I saw Edward Schroder.

SCHRODER moves forward.

SCHRODER: Good evening, Mr Fenton. I trust you had a pleasant journey.

FENTON: (*Surprised*) Dr Schroder!

SCHRODER: Not <u>Dr</u> Schroder, if you don't mind. I stopped using that title several months ago. You may remember the occasion.

FENTON: Oh, yes. Yes, I remember. There was a girl …

SCHRODER: (*Nodding; closing the subject*) There was a girl, Mr Fenton. (*To WADE; with authority*) Have you told the Sister?

WADE: Yes.

SCHRODER: Then tell Davis. Mr Fenton, a friend of ours has been taken ill. I examined him this morning and my diagnosis is that he is suffering from an acute volvulus. I'm quite convinced that an immediate operation is imperative. I want you to examine the patient and, providing of course you confirm my diagnosis, perform the operation.

FENTON: But why wasn't the patient sent to a
               hospital? If you examined him this morning
               …
SCHRODER: (*Interrupting FENTON*) It was not
               considered expedient.
FENTON: And supposing I refuse to operate?
SCHRODER: You won't, Mr Fenton, not when you have
               examined the patient.

The door opens.

SCHRODER: Ah!

*The NURSE and LINDA BROOKS wheel the patient into the
room on an operating table.*

*LINDA is an attractive girl in her late twenties, she is in full
white and wears a surgical mask which partly conceals her
face.*

*The MAN on the operating table is obviously in pain and is
delirious. He keeps repeating the words "… Golden Valley
…"*

*FENTON moves to the side of the patient and stands looking
down at him.*

MAN: (*Delirious*) … Golden Valley …

*FENTON looks up and catches LINDA's eye. FENTON
stares at her – their eyes meet.*

*After a moment FENTON lowers his eyes and looks down at
the patient again.*

MAN: … Golden Valley …
FENTON: (*To SCHRODER*) He keeps saying Golden
               Valley … What does he mean?

SCHRODER shrugs.

SCHRODER: He's delirious. He's been like this since six
           o'clock.
FENTON: All right. Let's take a look at him.

FENTON moves the sheet from the patient.

FENTON's voice: It took only a brief examination to confirm that Schroder was right. The man was suffering from an acute volvulus and I was pretty sure that an immediate operation was imperative.

CUT TO: The same room. Later.
FENTON is taking off his jacket and rolling up his sleeves in preparation for the operation.
The NURSE crosses behind him and pours hot water into the bowl on the side table.
FENTON turns, washes his hands, and accepts a small towel from the NURSE.
Still drying his hands on the towel he turns and looks down at the patient.
The MAN is still delirious.
FENTON suddenly frowns, and with a surprised expression looks up at WADE and SCHRODER.
FENTON's voice: It was only when I looked at the man for a second time that I recognised him. I'd operated on him two years ago at St Mathew's Hospital. It was Sir Oliver Peters!
FENTON stands staring down at PETERS.
He looks up at SCHRODER who meets his gaze.
LINDA touches FENTON's arm and he turns away from the table and notices that she is laying out surgical implements together with bandages, rubber gloves, etc, on the side table.
FENTON picks up the rubber gloves and is helped into a white coat.

CUT TO: The same. Later.
SCHRODER is taking off his surgical mask.

FENTON watches the patient being wheeled out of the room.

WADE rises from an armchair in the corner and comes across to FENTON and SCHRODER.

Both FENTON and SCHRODER look tired.

SCHRODER takes out his cigarette case and offers FENTON a cigarette.

FENTON hesitates, then accepts one.

WADE joins FENTON and offers him a light.

WADE: (*To SCHRODER*) Well?

SCHRODER: (*With a little shrug*) We shall see.

WADE: (*Irritated*) Yes, but is he going to be all right? Are you satisfied?

SCHRODER: Ask Mr Fenton, he performed the operation.

WADE looks at FENTON.

FENTON: Providing there are no complications he's got a chance.

WADE: What do you mean, a chance?

SCHRODER: (*Quietly, to WADE*) He'll be all right.

WADE: (*Satisfied*) Good! Well, let's have a drink. (*To FENTON*) You've earned it, my dear fellow.

WADE crosses to the drinks.

FENTON sits.

SCHRODER looks down at him.

SCHRODER: Did you recognise him?

FENTON: Yes. I recognised him. It's Sir Oliver Peters.

SCHRODER nods.

FENTON: The newspapers said he was in Moscow.

WADE brings drinks to FENTON and SCHRODER.

WADE: Which only goes to show how mistaken they can be. Here's your drink, Mr Fenton.

FENTON takes the drink from WADE.

FENTON: I don't pretend to know what this is all about, but I warn you that immediately I get back to town …

WADE: (*Interrupting FENTON*) Immediately you get back to town, my dear fellow, you can tell your friends – that you were kidnapped, taken to a country house, and told to operate on Sir Oliver Peters. (*Smiling*) They won't believe you, of course, but it'll make an interesting story.

FENTON looks at WADE, then drinks – he empties his glass.

He looks at the glass as he finishes the drink.

SCHRODER: (*To FENTON*) I believe you operated on Peters once before?

FENTON: Yes.

SCHRODER: When was that?

FENTON: April, 1950.

WADE takes FENTON's glass. He is watching him.

WADE: Let me get you another drink.

FENTON: No, thank you.

FENTON rises, hesitates, then sinks back onto the arm of the chair.

WADE: (*Quietly*) What is it?

FENTON: (*Slowly; puzzled*) I don't know. I feel very peculiar. It's almost as if my head … was …

FENTON puts his head in his hands.

SCHRODER looks across at WADE.

FENTON: Did … you … put something … in … my … drink …?

WADE: No, of course not, my dear fellow!

FENTON makes a determined effort and rises from the chair; he crosses the room and then suddenly collapses. SCHRODER catches him.

21

WADE looks across at SCHRODER and nods.

CUT TO: The Drawing Room of FENTON's Flat.
WYMAN and the INSPECTOR are listening to FENTON who continues his story.
FENTON is sitting opposite them.

FENTON: I knew that they'd drugged me but there was just nothing I could do about it. I passed completely out. They must have brought me back to Town in the ambulance because when I came round I found I was sitting on a bench in St James's Park. It was ten o'clock in the morning; just sixteen hours after they'd picked me up in Cranley Street. I had a headache and I felt tired, but apart from that I wasn't feeling too bad. I don't know how long I'd been in the park, I've a feeling it must have been an hour or so. I decided the best thing I could do was to go to the hospital.

CUT TO: Outside St Mathew's Hospital.
FENTON climbs the steps up to the entrance of the hospital. He is wearing his outdoor clothes (the clothes he was wearing when he was picked up by the ambulance).

FENTON's voice: As I entered the hospital I remember what Wade had said, and I realised that he was right. It was an incredible story and no one would believe me.

CUT TO: FENTON's Office. Day.
DR ANDREW SEFTON, a good-looking man in his early thirties, is standing by the desk reading an article in a medical magazine.
The door opens and FENTON enters.

22

SEFTON: (*Surprised*) Why, hello, Mark! We've been trying to get you on the phone. Where the Dickens have you been?

FENTON: (*Hesitating*) I – I had rather a late night.

SEFTON: Yes, by George, you look like it.

FENTON: What's all the fuss about anyway? I'm not supposed to be on duty today.

SEFTON: Yes, I know, old boy, but Gillespie asked me to get in touch. You may have to operate on 17.

FENTON: Oh?

SEFTON: Gillespie's not too happy about him.

FENTON: Gillespie's never happy about anything!

SEFTON: I say, you are in a bad way, Mark! Is anything the matter?

FENTON is agitated, uncertain whether to confide in SEFTON or not.

FENTON: Andrew, we've known one another a very long time, haven't we?

SEFTON: A very long time, old boy. Since prep school days.

FENTON: Well, look, Andrew, something happened to me last night. Something so – well – so fantastic that I just …

FENTON takes a carton of cigarettes from his pocket.

SEFTON: What is it?

FENTON stares at the packet of cigarettes.

FENTON: That's funny! Someone must have put this packet of cigarettes in my pocket.

SEFTON: What do you mean?

FENTON: I don't smoke these. I've never seen this packet before.

SEFTON: What are they?

FENTON looks at the packet of cigarettes.

FENTON: 'Mercury' … That's a new one on me.

23

SEFTON: Yes.

FENTON: They look American …

SEFTON: (*Amused*) You probably bought them last night and forgot about it.

FENTON: No, Andrew, I didn't because …

SEFTON: Well, probably the girl friend bought them.

There is a knock on the door and SISTER ROGERS enters.

FENTON: (*On edge*) Andrew, I didn't go out last night! At least I didn't … (*He stops, seeing SISTER ROGERS*)

SISTER: Excuse me, Mr Fenton. Dr Gillespie would like to see you, Dr Sefton. I think it's urgent, doctor. He's in Ward 2.

SEFTON: Yes, all right. I'll be up straight away.

SISTER ROGERS goes out.

SEFTON: (*To FENTON*) I'm afraid your story will have to wait, old boy.

FENTON: (*After a moment; resigned*) Yes, all right. I shall probably go back to the flat after lunch. If Gillespie wants me give me a ring.

SEFTON: O.K.

SEFTON starts heading for the door.

FENTON: (*Stopping SEFTON*) Oh, Andrew …

SEFTON: Yes?

FENTON: Do you remember that fellow you introduced me to at Sunningdale? The man we played golf with – Colonel something or other.

SEFTON: Colonel Wyman. Yes?

FENTON: Didn't you say he was attached to the Special Branch?

SEFTON: Did I? I thought he was with the Foreign Office or something.

FENTON: Well – what does he do exactly?

SEFTON: Good Lord, I haven't the slightest idea!
               He's quite a big bug, that's all I know.
               Look, I'll see you later, Mark! I can't stop
               now.

FENTON nods and SEFTON goes.

FENTON hesitates, then crosses the room.

He stops by the desk.

He puts his hand on the telephone, hesitates – almost changes his mind – then lifts the receiver.

FENTON: (*On the telephone*) This is Mr Fenton –
               Extension 95 … I want you to get me
               Scotland Yard … Yes … Ask for a Colonel
               Wyman … Yes, that's right, Wyman … Say
               it's Mr Fenton calling of St Mathew's
               Hospital … Oh, if you can't get Colonel
               Wyman at Scotland Yard try the Foreign
               Office … No, I'm afraid I don't know the
               number … Yes, I shall be here – ring me
               back … Thank you!

FENTON replaces the receiver then looks down at the carton of cigarettes which he is still holding.

CUT TO: The Front Door of FENTON's Flat. Late Afternoon.

FENTON's voice: I stayed at the hospital until late in the
               afternoon and then went to the flat to keep
               my appointment with Colonel Wyman. My
               appointment was for six o'clock, but it was
               about a quarter past five when I got to the
               flat. I found the door open.

CUT TO: The Drawing Room of FENTON's Flat.

EDWARD SCHRODER is sitting in the chair with his back to the camera. He is rather agitated.

25

FENTON enters.

FENTON: Schroder! What are you doing here?

SCHRODER: (*Tensely*) I thought you were never coming! I've been here since three o'clock.

FENTON: What's happened? Is Peters …

SCHRODER: (*Shaking his head*) He's all right. He regained consciousness and appears to be on the mend. Here's your key. I took it from your pocket this morning.

FENTON: Oh! I wondered what had happened to it.

SCHRODER: You did a pretty good job on Peters, Fenton. My God, it was touch and go. It's a good thing we sent for you.

FENTON: (*Angrily*) 'Sent' is hardly the right word, Dr Schroder!

FENTON makes a movement towards the bedroom.

SCHRODER: (*Quickly*) What are you going to do?

FENTON: I'm going to telephone the police; tell them you're here, and tell them exactly what happened last night!

SCHRODER: Wait! Wait a moment!

FENTON hesitates.

SCHRODER: Telephoning the police won't help you. If you tell them about Peters ten to one they won't believe you and in any case … (*A shrug*) your life will still be in danger.

FENTON: What do you mean – my life will still be in danger?

SCHRODER: Why do you think I came here this afternoon?

FENTON: I've no idea.

SCHRODER: I came to warn you. You've got to go away, Fenton. You've got to disappear, today,

26

now, otherwise … (*Facing FENTON; very serious*) Otherwise it may be too late.

FENTON: Are you crazy? Why should I disappear? (*Annoyed*) Now listen, Schroder …

SCHRODER: (*Interrupting FENTON; quietly, yet with authority*) Fenton, I don't think you quite understand the situation. I took a risk in coming here this afternoon but I took it because – well, because I thought you might have the common sense to listen to what I've got to say.

FENTON: (*Quietly*) Go on …

SCHRODER: You're not supposed to be here, Mr Fenton. You're supposed to be – dead.

FENTON: (*Shaken*) What do you mean?

SCHRODER: I'll explain what I can. After the operation, when Wade … But first, have you got a drink, Fenton – and a cigarette?

FENTON hesitates; undecided whether to trust SCHRODER or not.

After a moment he decides to do so.

FENTON: What would you like – whisky?

SCHRODER: If you've brandy, I … I should prefer it.

FENTON: Yes, all right.

FENTON turns away from SCHRODER, then hesitates and takes the carton of cigarettes out of his pocket. He throws the carton onto the desk.

FENTON: Oh, here's the cigarettes. (*He looks at SCHRODER*) I don't know whether you smoke this particular brand.

FENTON goes into the kitchen.

SCHRODER stares down at the desk.

He picks up the carton of cigarettes, holds it in his hand.

He looks puzzled; he turns and looks towards the kitchen.

27

CUT TO: FENTON's Kitchen.

FENTON opens the cupboard and takes out an unopened bottle of brandy.

He takes the tin-foil off the top of the bottle, then opens a drawer and takes out a corkscrew.

FENTON is just about to use the corkscrew when there is the sound of a revolver shot and the sudden smashing of glass.

He turns quickly, instinctively, towards the drawing room.

CUT TO: The Drawing Room in FENTON's Flat.

The body of EDWARD SCHRODER is on the floor in front of the large bay window.

A pane of glass is broken, having been shattered by the bullet which killed Schroder.

The carton of cigarettes is on the floor by the side of the body.

FENTON comes into the room and walks slowly towards him.

He lifts the packet of cigarettes.

CUT TO: The Drawing Room in FENTON's Flat.

COLONEL WYMAN and AUSTIN are listening to FENTON continue with his story.

FENTON: … At first I couldn't understand why the packet of cigarettes was by the side of the body and then I realised of course that Schroder must have picked the packet up off the desk. A policeman heard the shot and came up here to investigate. I refused to say anything and he phoned Scotland Yard. A quarter of an hour later you arrived, Inspector.

AUSTIN: And that's the whole story, Mr Fenton?

FENTON: Yes, the whole story.

AUSTIN looks at COLONEL WYMAN; his expression denoting extreme scepticism.

AUSTIN: I'm rather interested in this man Wade – the man in the ambulance. You say he had an Irish accent and was well dressed?

FENTON: Yes.

AUSTIN: How old would he be?

FENTON: Oh, it's difficult to say. Forty perhaps …

AUSTIN: M'm. This place they took you to, Mr Fenton – the place where according to your story, you performed the operation. Was it a country house?

FENTON: I only saw the one room, but that was my impression.

AUSTIN: Have you any idea where it was?

FENTON: No. We seemed to be in the ambulance for hours. I'm afraid that's all I can tell you.

AUSTIN: What do you mean hours? Two hours, three hours?

FENTON: I should say three hours at least.

AUSTIN: I see.

WYMAN: (*Quietly*) Mr Fenton …

FENTON turns towards WYMAN.

FENTON: Yes?

WYMAN: What was it Sir Oliver Peters said … "Golden Valley …"?

FENTON: Yes – Golden Valley …

WYMAN: You've no idea what he meant? What he was referring to?

The telephone rings.

FENTON: Not the slightest.

AUSTIN looks across at WYMAN.

FENTON: I expect that's the hospital. Will you excuse me?

29

WYMAN nods.

FENTON leaves AUSTIN and WYMAN in order to answer the telephone.

AUSTIN: Well, that's quite a story. It doesn't sound a very likely one to me, but if he is telling the truth then this looks like being your pigeon, thank God, and not ours!

WYMAN looks at the INSPECTOR but makes no comment.

He turns and crosses to the body of SCHRODER.

He stands looking down at SCHRODER.

FENTON's voice: (*On the telephone, in the background*) Yes, speaking … Oh, hello, Andrew … Yes … When? … I see … Yes, all right, old boy … No, don't worry about it …

WYMAN indicates the cigarette carton by the side of the body.

WYMAN: Do you mind if I take a look at this?

AUSTIN: (*After a moment*) No, carry on.

WYMAN picks up the cigarette packet and turns it over in his hand.

We hear the telephone receiver being replaced.

FENTON returns.

FENTON: (*To AUSTIN*) I'm afraid I've got to report to the hospital for an emergency operation. If you want me I shall be back here about eleven o'clock.

AUSTIN hesitates, then makes his mind up.

AUSTIN: Yes, all right, Mr Fenton.

FENTON looks at WYMAN, hesitates, then goes into the bedroom.

WYMAN watches him but makes no comment.

He looks down at the cigarette carton again; takes a different pair of glasses from his breast pocket and replaces the old pair in its case.

AUSTIN: (*Looking at the carton in Wyman's hand*) 'Mercury' cigarettes. I know most American brands but I've never heard of that one before.

WYMAN: Neither have I, Inspector.

WYMAN opens the packet of cigarettes.

He takes out a cigarette and looks at it.

He looks up at the Inspector.

WYMAN: That's curious.

AUSTIN: What is it?

WYMAN: It says 'Mercury' on the packet but the cigarettes are just ordinary Players.

WYMAN holds the cigarette up and looks at AUSTIN.

CUT TO: FENTON's Office. Night.

FENTON is standing near the desk examining an X-ray photograph. He is dressed in his surgical clothes.

The door opens and DR SEFTON enters.

He stands almost in the doorway, his hand on the handle of the door.

SEFTON: We shan't want you for about a quarter of an hour, Mark.

FENTON: (*Looking up*) Yes, all right. Has Thompson arrived?

SEFTON: Yes, he's with the patient.

FENTON: How does he seem?

SEFTON: Not too bad. I've given him an anaesthetic.

FENTON: Good.

SEFTON: Sorry we had to drag you back, old boy.

FENTON: Can't be helped.

FENTON looks at the X-ray again.

ROBIN TERRY appears in the doorway.

He is carrying a small oil painting.

ROBIN: (*To SEFTON*) Do you think I could have a word with Mr Fenton?

31

SEFTON: Yes, I think so.

FENTON: (*Looking up at the sound of ROBIN's voice*) Oh, hello, Mr Terry! Come in!

TERRY enters the room.

SEFTON nods to FENTON and goes out, closing the door.

FENTON: Has your mother left?

ROBIN: Not yet. She's still getting her things together. She'd like to see you before she leaves, Mr Fenton, if that's possible.

FENTON glances at his watch.

FENTON: Yes, of course.

ROBIN: You've been awfully kind to Mardie while she's been here. We're both terribly grateful.

FENTON: Well, she's been a pretty good patient, Mr Terry. I didn't think she was going to be, not at first but …

ROBIN: (*Laughing*) No, I'll bet you didn't! Do you know how many notes she sent me the first day she arrived?

FENTON: No?

ROBIN: Fourteen!

They laugh.

ROBIN: Mr Fenton, this is a painting of mine. It's just a little thing but I thought perhaps … (*A shade embarrassed*) Well, you really have been awfully kind to Mardie and I thought perhaps you might like to have it. (*With a sudden smile*) Providing you approve, of course!

FENTON laughs.

ROBIN holds the picture up, on the desk.

It is obvious that FENTON likes the picture.

FENTON: But I think that's enchanting! It's quite different from the other one you showed us.

ROBIN: (*Faintly amused*) Yes, it's – quite different. (*Smiling*) Well, you did say you like your trees to look like trees.

FENTON: (*Laughing*) Yes. Yes, I do indeed. (*Looking at the picture*) But this is charming …

ROBIN: I painted it two years ago when I was staying in the Cotswolds. It's a little place called Charlesworth.

FENTON: It looks a lovely spot.

ROBIN: Yes, it is. The trees stretch right down the side of the hill, almost into the village.

FENTON: What did you say they called it?

ROBIN: Charlesworth. It's a heavenly little place. It's about ten miles from Cirencester.

FENTON: Charlesworth? It's a nice name …

ROBIN: Yes. I believe the local people call it the Golden Valley …

FENTON's expression suddenly changes; he looks puzzled and serious.

END OF EPISODE ONE

EPISODE TWO

TWO DOZEN
CARNATIONS

OPEN TO: MARK FENTON's Office.

MARK FENTON and ROBIN TERRY are looking at the small oil painting.

ROBIN: I painted it two years ago when I was staying in the Cotswolds. It's a little place called Charlesworth.

FENTON: It looks a lovely spot.

ROBIN: Yes, it is. The trees stretch right down the side of the hill, almost into the village.

FENTON: What did you say they called it?

ROBIN: Charlesworth. It's a heavenly little place. It's about ten miles from Cirencester.

FENTON: Charlesworth? It's a nice name …

ROBIN: Yes. I believe the local people call it the Golden Valley …

FENTON: The Golden Valley …?

ROBIN: Yes.

There is a slight pause.

FENTON is staring at the picture; he is obviously puzzled.

ROBIN: (*Faintly embarrassed*) I say, do you really like it?

FENTON: (*Turning*) M'm? (*Suddenly*) Oh yes. Yes, I like it enormously.

ROBIN: (*Amused*) Because if you don't, old boy – you've only got to say so.

FENTON: No, really, I – I think it's delightful. When were you at Charlesworth last?

ROBIN: I haven't been there for about two years, not since I painted the picture. I've always meant to go back, but – well – you know how it is.

FENTON: Yes. How far would it be – from Town, I mean?

ROBIN: Oh, about a hundred miles I should imagine.

SEFTON enters.

SEFTON:	(*To ROBIN*) Excuse me. (*To FENTON*) We're ready now, Mark. Gillespie's in the theatre.
FENTON:	All right, Andrew. I'll be right up. (*To ROBIN*) Thank you, Mr Terry. It's very kind of you – it's a very nice picture. Now if you'll excuse me I must go.
ROBIN:	Yes of course. I'll pop upstairs and see how mother's getting on.

FENTON and TERRY go out.

CUT TO:	FENTON's Office. Later.

SISTER ROGERS is listening to a programme on the radio.

ANNOUNCER:	(*From the radio*) A Foreign Office spokesman confirmed that there is no definite information concerning the whereabouts of Sir Oliver Peters, the missing British diplomat. Reports from Bucharest that Sir Oliver has arrived in Moscow are entirely without foundation. (*Pause*) The Board of Trade has issued a statement concerning the present system of price control applying to wholesale and retail …

SISTER ROGERS switches the radio off.
She returns to the desk as DR SEFTON enters.
He looks worried.

SISTER:	Is the operation over?
SEFTON:	(*Rather curtly*) Yes.
SISTER:	Was everything all right, doctor?
SEFTON:	(*Shaking his head*) I'm not too happy. There was a moment when it was touch and go.
SISTER:	Oh, dear. What does Dr Gillespie think?

SEFTON: I don't know. Who's on duty tonight, Sister, in Ward 2?

SISTER: I am. (*She looks at her watch*) I take over at nine o'clock.

SEFTON: I think I'd have a word with Dr Gillespie, if I were you.

SISTER ROGERS picks up her paperwork.

SISTER: Yes, all right. Oh, by the way – perhaps you'd tell Mr Fenton there was a message for him from a Colonel Wyman.

FENTON appears in the doorway; he looks tired.

SEFTON: (*Surprised*) Colonel Wyman?

SISTER: Yes.

FENTON: What's that, Sister?

SISTER: Oh, there was a phone call for you, sir, from a Colonel Wyman. He said he was calling round to see you.

FENTON: Did he say what time he was calling?

SISTER: No, I'm afraid he didn't.

FENTON: I see.

SISTER: There's a note from Mrs Terry on the desk. She'd like to see you before she leaves.

FENTON: Oh, yes! I was forgetting Mrs Terry. Thank you, Sister.

SISTER ROGERS goes out.

FENTON picks up MRS TERRY's note, looks at it, then throws it down on the desk.

FENTON: (*To SEFTON*) I've told Gillespie to keep a very close eye during the night.

SEFTON: Yes, I think that's a wise precaution.

FENTON: What do you think, Andrew? Will he pull through?

SEFTON: He'll be all right providing there are no setbacks in the next twenty-four hours.

FENTON: Yes. Well, there's nothing more we can do, we shall just have to wait and see.

FENTON moves the papers on his desk.

FENTON: I wasn't exactly brilliant tonight, was I?

SEFTON makes no comment.

FENTON: Have you eaten yet?

SEFTON: No, I shall probably eat later. I thought of popping round to Oscar's.

FENTON: (*Looking at his watch*) I'll join you, Andrew, about nine o'clock.

SEFTON: Yes, all right.

SEFTON moves towards the door, then hesitates.

SEFTON: Mark …

FENTON: (*Looking up from his desk*) Yes?

SEFTON: What happened tonight?

FENTON: (*Vaguely*) Oh, it was just one of those things.

FENTON crosses the room.

FENTON: I felt on edge. Terribly on edge. There was nothing I could do about it.

FENTON takes out his cigarette case; then changes his mind and replaces it.

SEFTON: Mark, what is it? What's happened?

FENTON: Andrew, something happened to me last night. It's so fantastic but I've got to tell someone about it, otherwise I shall go crazy. When I left the hospital yesterday I was picked up by an ambulance. They took me to …

SEFTON: What do you mean – picked up?

FENTON: Well, it's difficult to explain, Andrew. I was walking back to the flat, and I'd just reached Cranley Street – you know – it's just off the Harrington Road – when suddenly … an ambulance drew up.

FENTON stops and turns towards the door.

40

COLONEL WYMAN is standing there.

WYMAN: Good evening, Mr Fenton. Did you get my telephone message?

FENTON: Yes. Yes, I did. Come in, Colonel!

WYMAN crosses towards FENTON.

WYMAN: (*To SEFTON*) Good evening!

FENTON: You know Dr Sefton, of course?

WYMAN: Yes, rather – we played golf together. Have you been to Sunningdale recently?

SEFTON: I was there a fortnight ago. (*A tiny pause*) It was very pleasant.

WYMAN: Yes, yes, I'm sure.

A pause.

SEFTON looks at WYMAN, then at FENTON.

SEFTON: Well – I'll see you later, Mark.

FENTON: Yes, all right.

SEFTON: (*To WYMAN*) Goodbye, sir.

WYMAN: Goodbye, doctor.

SEFTON leaves.

FENTON: Do sit down. Well, Colonel?

WYMAN: I thought you might like to know that Inspector Austin is now convinced that you were telling the truth – about the murder, I mean.

FENTON: What convinced him?

WYMAN: It's been established that the shot that killed Schroder was fired from the roof of a house opposite your flat. Incidentally, it's the Inspector's opinion that the shot was not intended for Schroder, but for you – however that's not important.

FENTON: I'm glad you think so.

WYMAN: (*Smiling*) No, you misunderstand me. I mean, the Inspector's opinion is not important. Mr Fenton, I'm going to ask you a question, and if

41

there's any doubt in your mind about the answer – even a flicker of doubt – please don't hesitate to say so!

FENTON: Well?

WYMAN: Are you quite convinced that the man you operated on was Sir Oliver Peters?

FENTON: Quite convinced. In any case they admitted it was Peters.

WYMAN: Yes, I know that. But did you actually recognise Peters before anyone mentioned his name?

FENTON: Yes. There's no doubt in my mind – none whatsoever. It was Sir Oliver Peters!

WYMAN: (*Nodding*) Right! Now tell me about the other people you saw at the house, beside Wade and Peters.

FENTON: Well – there was Schroder ...

WYMAN nods.

FENTON: ... the nurse who stopped me in the street ... and the other girl, the one who assisted at the operation.

WYMAN: Would you recognise them again?

FENTON: I'd recognise the nurse again, but the other girl was wearing a surgical mask all the time and she never actually spoke. I ... I doubt whether I'd recognise her.

WYMAN: Now about the place itself, the house I mean ...

FENTON: (*Suddenly*) Wait a minute! You remember I told you that Peters was delirious and that he kept saying ... the Golden Valley ...

WYMAN: Yes ...

FENTON: Well, I think he was trying to tell me where the place was, because I found out that the Golden Valley ...

WYMAN: (*Interrupting FENTON*) Is in the Cotswolds, about ten or twelve miles from Cirencester.

FENTON: Yes. (*Surprised*) It hasn't taken you long to find that out!

WYMAN: It wasn't really very difficult. Peters used to have a house in that part of the country – he only sold it eighteen months ago.

FENTON: I see.

WYMAN: (*Smiling*) But how did you find out about the Golden Valley?

FENTON turns towards the picture on the desk.

FENTON: Well, by a curious coincidence, when I got back to the hospital an artistic friend of mine – well, he's hardly a friend, he's the son of one of my patients – made me a present of this picture. I asked him where he'd painted it and he said in the Cotswolds at a place called Charlesworth. He said the local people always refer to Charlesworth as the Golden Valley.

WYMAN: I see. What's his name, this artist friend of yours?

FENTON: Robin Terry. Which reminds me, I really ought to be upstairs saying goodbye to his mother – she's leaving us tonight.

WYMAN: Is that why he gave you the picture?

FENTON: (*Rather resenting the question*) Yes, I suppose it is. She's been with us for six weeks.

WYMAN picks up the painting: takes out his spectacles case and changes his glasses.

He holds the picture away from him and looks at it.

A pause.

WYMAN: The young man certainly can paint.

WYMAN puts the picture down on the desk and takes off his glasses.

43

WYMAN: Mr Fenton, I'm going up to the Cotswolds for two or three days. I'm leaving tonight on the nine-fifteen. I may not be back in Town until Tuesday. If you should want to get in touch with me my number is Western 4532. If it's urgent leave a message for me.

FENTON: Yes, all right. Now if you'll excuse me.

WYMAN: (*Stopping FENTON*) I should make a note of the number. Western 4532.

FENTON: I don't imagine I shall want to get in touch with you, Colonel, but I'll …

WYMAN: (*Interrupting FENTON*) You might, Mr Fenton!

FENTON: (*Turning; surprised by WYMAN's tone of voice*) Why?

WYMAN: I don't want to be an alarmist but I think Schroder was telling you the truth this afternoon. Unless we find Sir Oliver Peters – and find him pretty quickly – your life is in danger.

FENTON: But that's absurd! This Peters business hasn't really anything to do with me. I was made to perform an operation. If I hadn't operated the man would have died. So far as I'm concerned that's all there is to it.

WYMAN: Not quite all. Do you remember the packet of cigarettes – the ones you found in your pocket?

FENTON: Yes.

WYMAN: The name on the packet was 'Mercury' – it looked like a carton of American cigarettes but the cigarettes themselves were just ordinary English cigarettes.

FENTON: Are you sure?

44

WYMAN: Quite sure. Those cigarettes were planted on you, and I believe that Schroder was surprised – very surprised – when you produced them.

FENTON: (*Bewildered*) Perhaps he was, but – I'm afraid I don't get this. What's the point?

WYMAN: Until you see the point, Mr Fenton, you can't say, with any assurance, that you've got nothing whatever to do with this affair.

WYMAN takes out his pocket watch and peers at it.

WYMAN: I'm afraid I shall have to go or I shall miss my train.

WYMAN turns: his eye catches the picture on the desk.
He lifts it up: puts on his glasses and stares at it.
A pause.

WYMAN: Yes – that young man certainly can paint.

WYMAN takes off his glasses and changes them.

CUT TO: A Private Room at St Mathew's Hospital.
MRS TERRY is preparing to leave.
A NURSE is busy changing the bedclothes and rearranging the bed.
MRS TERRY, assisted by LINDA BROOKS and SISTER ROGERS is collecting her various odds and ends and placing them in a small suitcase.
ROBIN is reclining in an armchair, taking no active part in the proceedings.

MRS TERRY: (*To SISTER*) Did you give my note to the Matron, Sister?

SISTER: (*Smiling*) Yes, I did, Mrs Terry – thank you.

MRS TERRY: Oh, and I sent a note to that nice girl – you know, the one with the protruding teeth and big hips.

ROBIN: She sounds very nice!

SISTER ROGERS and LINDA laugh.

MRS TERRY: She was sweet, she really was. Whenever I wanted anything she popped up here like a jack-in-the-box. Now where did I put my handbag?

SISTER ROGERS indicates the handbag.

SISTER: It's over here, Mrs Terry.

MRS TERRY: Oh, yes! I knew I'd left it somewhere.

MRS TERRY crosses and takes her handbag from the table.

MARK FENTON enters.

MRS TERRY: (*Delighted*) Oh, hello, Mr Fenton. How very nice of you to come and say goodbye.

FENTON: Not goodbye, Mrs Terry! I'm expecting you a week on Thursday at three o'clock. Now don't you forget!

MRS TERRY: I shan't, Mr Fenton, I promise you!

ROBIN: (*Laughing*) Hadn't you better make a note of it, Mardie?

MRS TERRY: You can laugh but my little notes have worked wonders in this hospital. Haven't they, Sister? Why, the first day I arrived everybody ignored me! Completely ignored me! I might just as well have been dead.

They all laugh.

MRS TERRY: Oh, before I forget, Mr Fenton. You remember the other day we were talking about art, and I said there was an awfully good book on the Pre-Raphaelites by a man called Berry?

FENTON: Yes.

MRS TERRY: Well, it wasn't Berry. I got the name and the title completely wrong.

ROBIN: (*Amused*) I suppose you mean Perry Brook's Life and the Pre-Raphaelites?

MRS TERRY takes a piece of paper out of her handbag.

MRS TERRY: That's it! Anyway, I've written it down for you, Mr Fenton.

MRS TERRY passes FENTON the note.

MRS TERRY: So you won't forget. Now do try and read it.

FENTON puts the note into his pocket.

FENTON: Yes, I will. (*To ROBIN*) And thank you again, Mr Terry, for the picture. I like it enormously.

MRS TERRY: Has Robin given you one of his pictures?

FENTON: Yes.

MRS TERRY: (*Suddenly*) Robin, I hope you didn't give Mr Fenton one of those horrible monstrosities!

ROBIN: No, Mardie, I didn't. I gave him a landscape – one I painted two years ago. (*To LINDA*) You remember the one, Linda. The picture I painted the … (*Suddenly; turning to FENTON*) Oh, I beg your pardon! I don't think you've met my fiancée!

FENTON: No, I don't think I have.

ROBIN: Linda, this is Mr Fenton. My fiancée – Miss Brooks.

FENTON shakes hands with LINDA.

FENTON: How do you do, Miss Brooks?

LINDA: How do you do, Mr Fenton? I've heard a great deal about you from Mrs Terry.

FENTON: (*Laughing*) Yes, I expect you have.

LINDA smiles at FENTON.

ROBIN looks at LINDA and FENTON.

ROBIN: (*Turning*) Well – are you ready, Mardie?

MRS TERRY: Yes – I've just got to close this case.

SISTER: Let me do it, Mrs Terry!

SISTER ROGERS joins MRS TERRY and closes the suitcase.

47

ROBIN: I'll take it down to the car.

ROBIN crosses and picks up the suitcase.

ROBIN: Well, goodbye, Mr Fenton! Goodbye, Sister!

SISTER: Goodbye, Mr Terry!

FENTON: (*Looking at LINDA*) Goodbye, Mr Terry.

ROBIN goes out.

MRS TERRY crosses to FENTON and holds out her hand.

MRS TERRY: Well, I'll say au-revoir, Mr Fenton. And again, many thanks.

FENTON: I'll see you on Thursday, Mrs Terry.

SISTER ROGERS crosses to MRS TERRY and FENTON.

MRS TERRY: (*Shaking hands with SISTER ROGERS*) Goodbye, Sister – and thanks for everything.

SISTER: Goodbye, Mrs Terry.

MRS TERRY crosses towards the door.

LINDA smiles at FENTON and then joins MRS TERRY.

She takes hold of MRS TERRY's arm as she is going through the door.

MRS TERRY: Now don't start taking hold of my arm! You'll make me feel a hundred. I haven't quite reached the bathchair stage – not yet!

LINDA turns and smiles at SISTER ROGERS.

LINDA and MRS TERRY leave.

FENTON stands watching the door.

SISTER: She's awfully good looking, isn't she?

FENTON: (*Turning*) Who? Mrs Terry?

SISTER: (*Giving FENTON "a look"*) No, not Mrs Terry. The fiancée – Miss Brooks.

FENTON: Yes, I suppose she is …

FENTON strokes his chain; he looks faintly puzzled.

CUT TO: OSCAR's Restaurant. Night.

This is a medium size, middle-class restaurant. There are numerous tables, wall settees, flowers, Italian prints on the walls, etc.

DR SEFTON is sitting at a table near the swing door.

OSCAR, an elderly waiter, brings SEFTON a plate of minestrone.

OSCAR: Here we are, doctor.

SEFTON: Thank you, Oscar.

OSCAR: Is Dr Fenton joining you tonight?

SEFTON: Yes, I think so. He said he was coming.

OSCAR: Good. Now what would you like to follow?

SEFTON: I'd like a steak!

OSCAR: I'm sorry, sir. I can recommend the plat du jour, sir.

SEFTON: (*Smiling*) Was there ever a day when you didn't recommend the plat du jour, Oscar? (*Nodding*) Yes, all right.

FENTON enters.

OSCAR: Good evening, Mr Fenton!

FENTON: Good evening, Oscar. Sorry I'm late, Andrew. I've been saying goodbye to Mrs Terry and her entourage. (*To OSCAR*) I'd like a large gin and French, Oscar – mostly gin.

OSCAR: Yes, sir.

OSCAR goes.

FENTON draws his chair up to the table.

FENTON: Andrew, did you meet that girl – the one Robin Terry's engaged to?

SEFTON: Yes, I did. She's pretty easy on the eye, isn't she?

FENTON: It's funny but I had the feeling I'd met her somewhere before.

49

SEFTON: You wouldn't forget a girl like that, old boy. At least, I wouldn't. I wonder what she sees in Terry. He strikes me as being frightfully dim.

FENTON: They probably have profound conversations about Salvador Dali.

SEFTON: Heaven forbid! I wonder if I could interest her in biology.

FENTON laughs.

FENTON: You keep away from Miss Brooks. I've got a feeling Robin Terry isn't quite as dim as he looks.

SEFTON: Well, he must have something. You're not going to kid me they talk art all the time!

FENTON laughs.

OSCAR brings FENTON his gin and French.

SEFTON drinks his soup.

A pause.

SEFTON: What did Colonel Wyman want, Mark?

FENTON: Oh – he just wanted to have a word with me about something.

SEFTON: Well, I rather imagined that. I didn't think he dropped in to have his appendix out.

SEFTON takes a roll from the basket on the table.

SEFTON: He's a curious bird, isn't he?

FENTON: Yes. How well do you know him?

SEFTON: Me? I hardly know him at all, old boy. We're members of the same golf club; we've had one game so far.

FENTON: I see.

SEFTON: (*Looking at FENTON*) How well do you know him, that's the point?

FENTON: (*Vaguely*) Oh – not very well – (*He hesitates*) I think he believed I'd murdered someone.

SEFTON: (*Putting down his spoon*) Murdered someone!

FENTON: Yes. Don't worry, he's since discovered that I didn't.

FENTON drinks, then puts down his glass.

FENTON: Do you remember Edward Schroder?

SEFTON: You mean the Austrian doctor who was mixed up in that awful scandal?

FENTON: Yes.

SEFTON: Of course I remember him. He was a brilliant fellow. Ought never to have got mixed up in that business.

FENTON: Well, he's dead.

SEFTON: What!

FENTON: He was shot – this evening. (*A moment*) In my flat.

SEFTON: Good Lord, no wonder you were jumpy tonight. But what happened? I didn't know Schroder was a friend of yours.

FENTON: He wasn't. I'd only met him once about three years ago at a Tanfield lecture.

SEFTON: Then what was he doing at your flat?

FENTON: He came to warn me. He told me to go away – to leave the country. He said my life was in danger.

SEFTON: But why on earth should he say that?

FENTON: Andrew, I know this sounds fantastic, but – when I left the hospital last night I was abducted and taken to a house somewhere in the country. I don't know for certain where the house was but I think it was in the Cotswolds.

SEFTON: What?

FENTON: The main room of the house was fitted up as an operating theatre and sitting in one of the armchairs, waiting for me, was Edward Schroder.

SEFTON: Go on, Mark.

FENTON: Schroder told me that they wanted me to
            perform an operation. The patient was brought
            in – he was a man of about sixty-five – and he
            was suffering from an acute volvulus. An
            immediate operation was imperative.

SEFTON: But who was the patient, why didn't they take
            him to a hospital?

FENTON: They couldn't.

SEFTON: Why not?

A pause.

FENTON: It was Sir Oliver Peters.

SEFTON: Sir Oliver Peters! The missing diplomat?

FENTON: Yes.

SEFTON: But – you must have been mistaken, Mark.
            Peters is in Moscow. Why every newspaper –

FENTON: (*Interrupting SEFTON*) I don't give a damn
            what the newspapers say! Peters is here – in
            this country. I operated on him twenty-four
            hours ago.

SEFTON: Good Lord! I just can't believe it. (*He looks up*)
            So that's why you got in touch with Wyman?

FENTON: Yes. I didn't know what to do.

SEFTON: But what happened? What happened after the
            operation?

OSCAR approaches the table.

FENTON: Well, after the operation was over the fellow
            who took me to the house – a man called Wade
            –

SEFTON: (*Turning to OSCAR*) Yes – what is it, Oscar?

OSCAR: (*To SEFTON*) Excuse me, sir. You're wanted
            on the telephone.

SEFTON: (*Annoyed*) T't! Who is it?

OSCAR: I don't know, sir – the gentleman just asked for Dr Sefton. It sounded like the hospital, sir.

SEFTON: Yes, all right. (*He rises; to FENTON*) Ten to one it's Gillespie! Do you know, this has happened three times this week! I'm sure he does it deliberately!

SEFTON puts his napkin down and leaves the table.

OSCAR: (*To FENTON*) Now what would you like, sir? I can recommend the plat du jour, Mr Fenton.

FENTON gives OSCAR a 'look'.

FENTON: Yes, all right, Oscar.

OSCAR goes.

A moment.

FENTON doesn't notice LINDA BROOKS approach the table.

LINDA: Mr Fenton!

FENTON: (*Surprised; rising*) Why, hello, Miss Brooks!

LINDA: I called at the hospital and they said you were probably here.

FENTON: Sit down, Miss Brooks! Do sit down!

LINDA hesitates; glances towards the door; then sits in SEFTON's place.

LINDA: I'm sorry if I've interrupted your dinner, but – (*She glances towards the door again*) I had to see you.

FENTON: Well, here I am!

LINDA: (*Quietly*) You recognised me, didn't you?

FENTON: (*Smiling*) Well, I know I've seen you somewhere before but I just can't place –

FENTON stops speaking; his expression suddenly changes. He has recognised LINDA.

LINDA: (*Softly*) Last night …

FENTON: (*Watching LINDA, slowly*) Yes, I remember now. You were the Sister. You wore a surgical mask, that's why I didn't recognise you.

LINDA: Yes. Mr Fenton, I've taken a great risk in coming here tonight. I wouldn't have done it, only …

FENTON: Only what?

LINDA: (*Leaning forward; across the table*) Edward Schroder risked his life for you. He needn't have gone to your flat, but he did. He went because he had an admiration for you and he … didn't want you to get drawn into this thing.

FENTON: What do you mean?

LINDA: Schroder told you to go away, didn't he? He told you to disappear.

FENTON: Yes.

LINDA: Well, you've got to disappear!

FENTON: (*Angrily*) How can I? I just can't vanish into thin air.

LINDA: If you don't, I warn you – they'll kill you. They'll kill you as sure as they killed Edward Schroder.

FENTON: Miss Brooks, look … I'm a surgeon at St Mathew's Hospital. I've got a job to do and a living to earn.

LINDA: (*Tensely*) But don't you realise you're in danger of losing your life!

FENTON: Do you mind if I ask you a question?

LINDA: Well?

FENTON: Who – and what – exactly, am I in danger from?

LINDA makes no reply.

FENTON: You see, your warning – and Dr Schroder's warning – doesn't make sense. I played in with

54

your people, didn't I? I did what I was told and performed the operation. It was your people, presumably, who brought me back to Town.

LINDA: (*Rather desperate; on edge*) Yes, but don't you understand they never intended to bring you back to Town. At least … (*Turning away*) Oh, what's the use.

LINDA rises.

FENTON: (*Quietly, but with authority*) Sit down.

FENTON rises and stands next to LINDA.

She hesitates.

FENTON: Sit down, Miss Brooks!

LINDA sits down.

FENTON stands looking down at her.

LINDA: (*Anxiously*) What are you going to do?

FENTON: I'll tell you what I'm going to do. I'm going to call a cab and take you down to Scotland Yard.

LINDA: (*Rising*) Scotland Yard!

FENTON: Yes. You know where that house is. You know where they took me to last night.

LINDA: What do you mean?

OSCAR's voice: (*Calling*) Mr Fenton! Mr Fenton, sir!

FENTON: You know where Sir Oliver Peters is and I haven't the slightest intention of letting you go until I find out.

OSCAR arrives at the table.

FENTON: What is it, Oscar?

OSCAR: It's Dr Sefton, sir! There's been an accident!

FENTON: An accident? What d'you mean?

OSCAR: I don't know what happened, sir! The doctor's in the telephone box. I think he's badly hurt, Mr Fenton!

FENTON gives a quick look at LINDA then rushes off with OSCAR.

55

CUT TO: A Telephone Box Alcove in the Restaurant.

DR SEFTON is down on one knee leaning against the wall, one hand holding the back of his head, the other over his eyes.

FENTON arrives, followed by OSCAR.

FENTON: (*Taking hold of SEFTON's arm*) Andrew, what is it? What's happened?

SEFTON slowly straightens himself, opens his eyes and looks at FENTON.

SEFTON: Someone hit me on the head while I was on the phone. (*In obvious pain*) I went down like a log. Fortunately I've got a pretty thick skull otherwise … I'd have had it …

OSCAR: But who was it, sir? Did you see the man?

SEFTON: No, I didn't. Naturally, I was standing with my back to the door. Oh, my head …

FENTON: Take it easy, Andrew …

SEFTON: (*To FENTON*) The funny thing is, I think the phone call was for you, Mark. When I answered it a man said is that Mr Fenton …

FENTON: Yes?

SEFTON: It wasn't the hospital. (*To OSCAR*) Get me a brandy, Oscar.

OSCAR: Yes, sir.

FENTON: Take it to the table.

OSCAR: Yes, sir.

OSCAR goes.

FENTON takes hold of SEFTON's arm and steadies him.

FENTON: Are you feeling any better?

SEFTON: Yes – I'll be all right.

FENTON: You know what happened, don't you?

SEFTON: What do you mean?

FENTON: Oscar thought the man on the phone said Sefton. He didn't – he said Fenton. This was

	intended for me. Not only the phone call but – what happened.
SEFTON:	(*Looks at FENTON*) You mean – someone mistook me for you?
FENTON:	That's my guess. Let's go back to the table.

CUT TO: The table in OSCAR's restaurant.

LINDA has departed.

FENTON and SEFTON arrive at the table.

FENTON looks about him: realises that LINDA has vanished.

FENTON: Sit down. I shan't be a minute!

FENTON dashes through the swing door in search of LINDA.

SEFTON sits at the table, holds his head and shakes it slightly.

OSCAR arrives with the brandy.

OSCAR:	Do you feel any better, sir?
SEFTON:	Yes, I'm nearly all right now.
OSCAR:	(*Puzzled*) What happened, sir? Did the man take your wallet?
SEFTON:	(*Feeling his pocket*) No. No, it's still here.
OSCAR:	(*Hesitantly*) Would you like me to send for the police, sir?
SEFTON:	(*Feeling his head*) No – don't worry about it, Oscar.

FENTON returns.

FENTON:	(*To OSCAR*) What happened to the young lady?
OSCAR:	I don't know, sir. She must have left.
SEFTON:	What young lady?
FENTON:	Linda Brooks was here.
SEFTON:	Linda Brooks!

FENTON: She came to the table while you were on the phone. (*Dismissing OSCAR*) It's all right, Oscar.

OSCAR goes.

FENTON: Andrew, I told you I thought I'd seen Miss Brooks somewhere before, didn't I?

SEFTON: Yes.

FENTON: She was at that house last night; she was there when I operated on Sir Oliver Peters.

SEFTON: Good Lord! Are you sure?

FENTON: Absolutely sure! In any case, she admitted it.

SEFTON: But why did she come here – to see you?

FENTON: Yes, she said I was in danger and she wanted to warn me. But I've got a shrewd suspicion that what she really wanted was to keep me talking while …

SEFTON: While I was on the telephone.

FENTON: Yes – and yet, that doesn't make sense, does it?

SEFTON: What do you mean?

FENTON: (*Thoughtfully*) You know, Andrew, I think she must have been telling me the truth after all. She knew about that phone call – she knew what would happen if I attempted to answer it.

SEFTON: Yes. (*After a moment*) Mark, if Linda Brooks is mixed up in this Peters affair, do you think Robin Terry is and his mother?

FENTON: I don't know about Mrs Terry, but Terry might be. What is it?

SEFTON: (*His hand on his nose*) My nose is beginning to bleed. Have you got a handkerchief?

FENTON: Yes, I've got a clean one somewhere.

FENTON feels in his pockets and finally produces a clean handkerchief; as he passes it to SEFTON, MRS TERRY's note falls on the table.

58

FENTON: Yes, here you are.

SEFTON: (*Taking the handkerchief*) Thanks.

A pause.

SEFTON puts the handkerchief to his nose.

SEFTON: You've dropped something.

FENTON: (*Picking up the note*) Oh yes. It's a note Mrs Terry gave me. It's the title of a book she wants me to read.

FENTON looks at the note.

FENTON: You know, Andrew, Linda Brooks may be mixed … (*He stops*)

SEFTON: What is it?

FENTON: (*Staring at the note*) That's funny! This isn't the title of a book.

SEFTON: Well – what is it? What does it say?

FENTON: (*Reading*) "Dear Mr Fenton … Imperative order two dozen carnations. White. Mayfair 1973 …"

SEFTON: (*Amused*) The silly old thing, she's given you the wrong note.

FENTON: (*Still looking at the note*) I'm not so sure. It's got today's date on it and it says … "Dear Mr Fenton" … (*He stares at it*) "Imperative order two dozen carnations" …

A pause.

FENTON rises from the table; he hesitates and looks at the note again.

SEFTON: What are you going to do?

FENTON: (*Matter of fact*) I'm going to order two dozen carnations …

FENTON walks away from the table.

CUT TO: A Telephone Box Alcove in the Restaurant.

FENTON arrives, lifts the receiver, puts a coin in the box and dials.

As he listens for the ringing tone, he looks about him, determined not to be taken unawares.

The ringing tone stops and he turns towards the telephone and presses button A.

FENTON: Hello? Is that Mayfair 1973? ... I ... want to order some flowers, please ... Yes, that's right ... Some flowers.

CUT TO: A Telephone mounted on a Wall.

WADE is speaking into a small telephone; he is holding a cigar in one hand. He looks very serious.

WADE: Who is it speaking? ... Well, who are you speaking for ... Mrs Terry? ... I see ... Well, what sort of flowers? ... Carnations? ... Yes ... What colour? ... I'm sorry, I didn't hear you ... Two dozen? ...Yes, I think we can manage that, but they've got to be collected ... You know that, of course ... No, I'm afraid it'll have to be tonight ... Oh, about eleven-thirty ... I'll give you the address. Room 5, the Polygon Club, Enden Street ... It's just off the Tottenham Court Road, not far from Warren Street tube station ... Yes, Polygon ... P-O-L-Y-G-O-N ... (*Politely*) That's right ... Thank you, sir.

WADE replaces the receiver; he thoughtfully puts the cigar in his mouth.

CUT TO: Enden Street. Night.

FENTON and SEFTON are walking down Enden Street. They stop under a street lamp and stare across the road.

FENTON: That's the place all right.

SEFTON: Yes.

SEFTON glances at his watch.

SEFTON: It's just half past.

FENTON: Give me ten minutes exactly, Andrew. If I'm not out in ten minutes you know what to do.

SEFTON: Yes, but I don't see why I can't come in with you. It's far better for two of us to …

FENTON: It's far better for one of us to be on the outside. It's probably a damn foolish thing to do anyway!

SEFTON: Well, I've already told you that, old boy. You ought to have contacted Wyman.

FENTON: Wyman's away – he's in the Cotswolds. Don't worry, Andrew – I'll be all right.

SEFTON looks at his watch again.

SEFTON: Ten minutes exactly.

FENTON nods.

He crosses the road to the entrance to the Polygon Club.

There is a sign saying "Members Only".

As FENTON walks to the door a girl is coming out.

1st GIRL: Hello, dear. You all alone?

FENTON ignores her and walks into the entrance hall.

The GIRL shrugs and walks off.

As FENTON gets to the foot of a staircase a coloured man and a girl come down the stairs and pass him.

As the man nears the camera he stops and looks back at FENTON, then moves off with the girl.

FENTON goes upstairs.

When he reaches the landing, MASON and a 3rd GIRL are kissing at the door of No 6.

The GIRL is trying to break away but MASON stops her.

JIMMY and a 4th GIRL come down some stairs.

JIMMY: Can't you find somewhere more comfortable?

MASON: We're quite comfy here. Aren't we, baby?

3rd GIRL: No, we're not! Let me go.

JIMMY: Cut it out, Arthur.

MASON: You mind your business, I'll mind mine.

JIMMY: Oh come on, leave the kid alone.

4th GIRL: You leave her alone, you great lout.

MASON: Beat it – both of you.

JIMMY: Okay, come on Alice.

JIMMY and the 4th GIRL go off.

MASON tries to kiss the girl again but she gets free and runs upstairs.

MASON goes after her.

FENTON has come up as JIMMY and the GIRL go off.

He sees No 5 and knocks on the door.

As he waits MASON and the GIRL have gone off and he is left alone.

He knocks again and when he gets no reply he opens the door and goes in.

CUT TO: Room No 5 in the Polygon Club

The room is over-furnished and very ornate; it looks like the headquarters of a "Professional" lady.

There are several pieces of furniture, including a settee which is in the centre of the room, and a large elaborate screen. There is a door obviously leading to a bedroom.

FENTON enters.

He closes the door behind him.

He is surprised and a little taken aback by the room.

He slowly crosses taking stock of his surroundings.

He moves in front of the settee, then suddenly stops.

He puts his arm on the arm of the settee, as if to steady himself.

The body of MRS TERRY is on the floor; she has obviously been murdered.

FENTON suddenly moves forward and kneels down by MRS TERRY.

She is staring up at the ceiling; there is blood at the corner of her mouth.

FENTON puts his arm under MRS TERRY, as if to move her, then suddenly hesitates.

He looks towards the door leading into the bedroom: he has obviously heard something.

He rises, glances quickly round the room and notices the screen.

He crosses and moves behind it.

A pause.

The bedroom door opens and COLONEL WYMAN comes out; he is carrying something in his hand and is in the process of changing his glasses.

He crosses and looks down at MRS TERRY: he adjusts his glasses.

After a moment he kneels down and carefully places the small object he is carrying by the side of the body.

It is a carton of 'Mercury' cigarettes.

END OF EPISODE TWO

EPISODE THREE

UNDER SUSPICION

OPEN TO: Room 5 at the Polygon Club.

COLONEL WYMAN is placing a carton of 'Mercury' cigarettes by the body of MRS TERRY.

He straightens himself; glances round the room; adjusts his glasses, then walks out of the room closing the door.

FENTON slowly reappears from behind the screen; he looks towards the door through which WYMAN has departed and then crosses and stands looking down at MRS TERRY.

He is obviously worried and puzzled; he looks round the room and notices a telephone on a small table in the corner.

He hesitates, then crosses to the phone, lifts the receiver and dials.

He listens to the ringing tone.

FENTON: (*On the phone*) Scotland Yard? … Send someone to the Polygon Club in Enden Street … Yes, straight away … (*Quietly*) Murder …

He holds the receiver away from him and looks across at MRS TERRY.

MAN's voice: (*On the other end of the line; from the receiver in FENTON's hand*) Who is that? … Who is that calling, please? … Hello? … Hello? … Can you hear me? … Who is that, please?

FENTON slowly replaces the receiver.

CUT TO: The Drawing Room in FENTON's flat. Night.

FENTON and SEFTON are in the room.

SEFTON stubs out a cigarette in an ashtray which is full of cigarette ends.

He is standing by the table. It is late at night and the curtains are drawn.

He is holding a drink in one hand; he looks serious.

The atmosphere is not exactly unfriendly, but certainly tense.

67

SEFTON: … It's a good job you didn't give your name. If you want my frank opinion, it wasn't very bright of you to phone the police!

FENTON: But Mrs Terry was dead, Andrew! She's been murdered … I had to phone them!

SEFTON: Listen, Mark, I don't think you realise just how tricky this situation is.

FENTON: What do you mean?

SEFTON: The police found the body of Edward Schroder here – in your flat. He'd been murdered. Correct?

FENTON: Yes.

SEFTON: By the side of the body they found a packet of cigarettes – 'Mercury' cigarettes.

FENTON: Well?

SEFTON: Those cigarettes belonged to you, Mark. You admitted – yourself – that you'd handed them to Schroder.

FENTON: (*Exasperated*) But I don't know where the cigarettes came from. I found them in my pocket after I'd operated on Peters.

SEFTON: Yes, I know. But the point is, the police will instinctively associate 'Mercury' cigarettes with the Schroder murder and with Mark Fenton.

FENTON: What do you mean?

SEFTON: They'll see the cigarettes by the body of Mrs Terry; they'll make inquiries; they'll find out that she was a patient of yours.

FENTON: Yes, but look here! If I wanted to murder Mrs Terry – or anyone else for that matter! – would I leave a packet of cigarettes, my cigarettes, by the side of the body? Of course I wouldn't! No, it's no use, Andrew. I've made up my mind.

68

I'm going down to the Yard first thing tomorrow morning to tell Austin exactly what happened.

SEFTON: (*Quietly*) What did happen?

FENTON: How do you mean?

SEFTON: Well – what did happen? What are you going to tell him?

FENTON: (*Annoyed*) I've told you. I'm going to tell him the truth!

SEFTON: That you received a note from Mrs Terry asking you to ring a certain number and order two dozen carnations?

FENTON: Yes.

SEFTON: That you phoned the number and that they sent you to the Polygon Club in Enden Street?

FENTON: Yes!

SEFTON: That when you got to the Club you discovered that Mrs Terry had been murdered and that you saw Colonel Wyman place a packet of 'Mercury' cigarettes by the body. (*A moment*) Is that what you're going to tell him, Mark?

A pause.

SEFTON: Well?

FENTON doesn't reply.

SEFTON: It doesn't sound a very likely story, does it?

FENTON: I don't give a damn whether it's a likely story or not, it's the truth!

SEFTON: It may be the truth, but if they don't believe it, where does that get you? Mark, don't you see, you're in a spot. I'm only trying to help you.

FENTON: (*Obviously worried*) Yes, I know that, Andrew.

SEFTON: And there's another thing, supposing Wyman says that he wasn't at the Polygon Club tonight?

69

FENTON: But he was!

SEFTON: Yes, I know. But supposing he says that he wasn't?

FENTON: In that case it's simply a question of his word against mine.

SEFTON: Exactly!

FENTON looks at SEFTON.

FENTON: Well, what would you do, if you were in my shoes?

SEFTON: I shouldn't tell them anything until they asked me, and when they asked me I should say, that after I'd left the hospital I went to Oscar's and we – that is you and I – had dinner together, and then we came back here.

The door bell rings.

SEFTON turns towards the alcove.

SEFTON: That's the front door bell.

FENTON: Yes.

FENTON glances at his watch.

FENTON: It's a quarter past one.

FENTON crosses towards the hall.

FENTON: Who the devil can it be?

FENTON goes out into the hall and opens the front door.

DETECTIVE-INSPECTOR AUSTIN is standing in the doorway.

He is wearing a trench coat and carries a trilby.

His coat is wet.

AUSTIN: Good evening, Mr Fenton. I'm sorry if I'm disturbing you.

FENTON: (*After a momentary hesitation*) Not at all, Inspector. Come in!

AUSTIN enters.

AUSTIN: I was afraid I might be getting you out of bed.

FENTON: No, no, as a matter of fact I'm entertaining a friend.

FENTON and AUSTIN enter the drawing room.

SEFTON is looking towards the alcove.

FENTON: This is a colleague of mine, Dr Sefton.

AUSTIN: Good evening.

FENTON: (*To SEFTON*) This is Detective-Inspector Austin, Andrew.

SEFTON: Oh! Good evening, Inspector!

FENTON: Would you like a drink, Inspector?

AUSTIN: No, thank you. (*He opens his coat*) It's rather late, Mr Fenton, so I'll come straight to the point. I believe you had a patient at the hospital called Mrs Terry – Mrs Beatrice Terry?

FENTON: That's right.

AUSTIN: Was she a friend of yours?

FENTON: No, just a patient.

SEFTON: Has anything happened to her?

AUSTIN: (*Turning towards SEFTON*) She's been murdered.

SEFTON: Murdered?

AUSTIN: We found Mrs Terry at the Polygon Club in Enden Street.

SEFTON: But – how was she murdered – exactly?

AUSTIN: (*Quite matter of fact*) Someone hit her on the back of the head, with what, I believe, is usually described as a blunt instrument.

FENTON: When did this happen?

AUSTIN: I should say, about eleven o'clock.

AUSTIN looks at SEFTON, then across at FENTON.

FENTON: Well, what can I do exactly?

AUSTIN: I don't know that you can do anything. We discovered that Mrs Terry was a patient of yours so naturally I thought – (*He glances at SEFTON*) I'd like to have a word with you.

There is a slightly awkward pause.

SEFTON: Well – I'll be making a move, Mark.

FENTON: Yes, all right, Andrew.

SEFTON picks up his hat and coat which is on a nearby chair.

AUSTIN: Let me help you on with your coat, doctor.

SEFTON: Oh, thank you.

AUSTIN takes SEFTON's coat and helps him on with it.

AUSTIN: (*Casually*) Have you been with Mr Fenton all evening?

SEFTON: Yes, we had dinner together at Oscar's – that's a little restaurant near the hospital.

AUSTIN: Yes, I know it.

SEFTON: Then we came back here. We've been here ever since. (*To FENTON*) That's right, isn't it, Mark?

FENTON looks a shade uncomfortable.

FENTON: Yes, that's right.

AUSTIN: What time was it when you left the restaurant?

FENTON: About ten fifteen. We got back here about a quarter to eleven.

AUSTIN: I see.

SEFTON: Well, I'll be off. I'll drop in tomorrow morning and pick you up, Mark.

FENTON: Yes, all right.

AUSTIN: (*To SEFTON*) I hope I'm not chasing you away?

SEFTON: (*Smiling*) Not you, Inspector. A guilty conscience.

SEFTON goes out through the alcove.

AUSTIN: He seems a very self-possessed young man.

FENTON: He's got to be, Inspector.

AUSTIN: Yes, I suppose so.

AUSTIN sits and takes out his pipe.

AUSTIN: Mr Fenton, you remember the packet of cigarettes we found by the body of Edward Schroder? 'Mercury' cigarettes.

FENTON sits.

FENTON: Yes, I remember.

AUSTIN: (*Sucking his pipe*) Well, there's rather a curious coincidence – we found a similar packet by the side of Mrs Terry. We've checked with her son – an artist fellow called Robin.

FENTON: Yes, I know Robin Terry.

AUSTIN: And he tells us that his mother was a non-smoker. In other words someone – presumably the murderer – must have deliberately planted the cigarettes there.

FENTON: Well?

AUSTIN: Well, according to your statement, Mr Fenton, you found the cigarettes in your pocket – the first packet, I mean – after you'd operated on Peters.

FENTON: Yes.

AUSTIN: (*Slowly*) Well now, I'm wondering if this Terry murder and the Schroder murder, couldn't in any way be connected with the disappearance of Sir Oliver Peters.

FENTON: (*Surprised*) Well, the Schroder murder definitely was.

AUSTIN: And Mrs Terry?

FENTON: I – wouldn't know about Mrs Terry.

AUSTIN: M'm.

FENTON: Have you any news of Sir Oliver Peters?

AUSTIN: Not a thing. Several of our people are in the Cotswolds but so far they've drawn a blank. By the way, Wyman told me about that picture, the one young Terry gave you of the Golden Valley. That was rather an odd coincidence, wasn't it?

FENTON: I thought so.

FENTON faces AUSTIN.

FENTON: That's why I told Colonel Wyman about it.

AUSTIN: Yes. Yes, of course.

FENTON: Inspector, how long has Colonel Wyman been a member of Scotland Yard?

AUSTIN: I couldn't say. He's attached to the Special Branch. I don't meet them very often. Why do you ask?

FENTON: I – I was curious, that's all.

AUSTIN: M'm. (*Changing the subject*) What do you make of Robin Terry?

FENTON: I've only met him two or three times. He seems quite a nice fellow. He's a very good artist.

AUSTIN: So I understand.

FENTON: Does he know – about – his mother?

AUSTIN: Yes. He was very distressed. We had quite a time with him. (*Hesitantly*) By the way, have you anything to tell me, Mr Fenton, about Mrs Terry?

FENTON: No.

AUSTIN: Nothing happened tonight, for instance?

FENTON: (*Tensely*) What do you mean?

AUSTIN: (*Quite friendly*) Well, she left the hospital, didn't she? Was she in good spirits?

FENTON: Oh, yes, very.

AUSTIN: I can't imagine what a woman like that was doing at the Polygon Club; apart from anything else it's hardly the sort of place you'd expect to find a semi-invalid. Don't you agree?

FENTON:	I don't know. I've never been to the Polygon Club.
AUSTIN:	No. No, of course not. Well, it's one of those places near the Tottenham Court Road. They get a lot of coloured boys there. They Jive or Be-bop or whatever it is.
FENTON:	It doesn't sound like Mrs Terry's cup of tea.
AUSTIN:	No.
FENTON:	Didn't her son give you any explanation?
AUSTIN:	(*Sucking his pipe; non-committally*) Er – no.

AUSTIN moves to the window.

AUSTIN:	Well, I suppose I'd better be making a move. I expect you want to get to bed.
FENTON:	I'm never very early.

AUSTIN moves the curtains and glances out of the window.

AUSTIN:	It's still raining, I see. It started to rain at half-past eleven; I remember looking at my watch.

AUSTIN turns and faces FENTON.

AUSTIN:	Half-past eleven, Mr Fenton.

CUT TO:	The Drawing Room of MARK FENTON's Flat. The following morning.

MRS DOBSON, the daily woman, comes out of the kitchen carrying a tray bearing coffee, milk, toast, a morning newspaper, etc.

She puts the tray down on the small table and then crosses to the bedroom door.

She knocks on the bedroom door.

MRS DOBSON: (*Calling*) Mr Fenton! Mr Fenton, your breakfast is ready!

FENTON: (*From inside the bedroom*) Yes, all right,
                 Mrs Dobson. I'll be out in a minute.

MRS DOBSON takes off her apron and rolls it up.

*She picks up her coat and hat off a nearby chair and puts
them on.*

*FENTON comes out of the bedroom; he is partly dressed,
but wears a dressing gown instead of his jacket.*

FENTON: Good morning, Mrs Dobson.

MRS DOBSON: Oh, good morning, sir! I've cleaned up the
                 mess in the kitchen an' I've done the
                 bathroom. Is there anything else you want,
                 Mr Fenton?

FENTON: No, I don't think so. Oh, the laundry seem
                 to be awfully slow these days, Mrs
                 Dobson, do you think you can do anything
                 about it?

MRS DOBSON: I can try, sir – but they're very
                 independent.

FENTON: Yes, I know.

MRS DOBSON: Do you know, my laundry bill last month
                 – including a few odds and ends of our
                 Edith's was two pounds eleven. I mean,
                 it's wicked, isn't it? It's just buying the
                 stuff back from 'em, that's all it is.

FENTON pours himself a cup of coffee.

A pause.

MRS DOBSON gives a little cough.

FENTON: (*Looking up; suddenly realising that MRS
                 DOBSON is about to leave*) Oh! I owe you
                 some money, don't I, Mrs Dobson?

MRS DOBSON: Yes, two pounds four and eight pence, sir.
                 That includes the soap and the toilet – er –

FENTON: (*Taking his wallet from his pocket*) Well –
                 here's three pounds. Keep the change and

76

I'll straighten things out with you next week.

The door bell rings.

MRS DOBSON: Yes, all right, doctor.

FENTON: See who that is. It's probably Dr Sefton.

MRS DOBSON goes out into the hall.

FENTON drinks his coffee.

We hear the sound of MRS DOBSON's voice talking to ROBIN TERRY.

MRS DOBSON returns.

MRS DOBSON: It's a Mr Terry, sir.

ROBIN TERRY enters: he looks tired and over-wrought.

FENTON: Oh, come in, Terry!

ROBIN: I hope I'm not interrupting your breakfast.

FENTON: Oh, that's all right.

FENTON looks at MRS DOBSON: obviously wishing that she would go.

MRS DOBSON: Well. I'll be off, Mr Fenton. I'll see what I can do about the laundry. Be better if they picked it up on a Thursday, wouldn't it?

FENTON: Yes, it would.

MRS DOBSON: Not so much messing about.

FENTON: (*Dismissing MRS DOBSON*) Well, just see what you can do.

MRS DOBSON: O.K. Tomorrow – same time?

FENTON: Yes.

MRS DOBSON: Goodbye.

FENTON: Goodbye, Mrs Dobson.

MRS DOBSON leaves.

ROBIN: I suppose you've heard about my – mother.

FENTON: Yes. The police came here last night. I'm terribly sorry. It must have been a dreadful shock for you. Do sit down.

77

ROBIN turns towards FENTON: bewildered.

ROBIN: I don't understand it. I've been awake all night. I've been trying to work out in my mind what happened – what possibly could have happened. There just doesn't seem to be an explanation.

FENTON: Well, there must be an explanation, Mr Terry.

ROBIN: Yes, but – what was my mother doing at a place like the Polygon Club? I went there this morning. After what the police told me I felt I had to see the place. It's a terrible place. A cheap, disreputable hole in the corner club that only – I don't understand. I just don't understand what my mother was doing at a place like that.

FENTON: (*Quietly*) What happened after you left the hospital last night?

ROBIN: What do you mean?

FENTON: Did you take your mother home?

ROBIN: Yes, of course. That's the extraordinary thing about it. She seemed in such good spirits. I don't remember seeing her so happy. We got home about half past eight. I stayed with her for about half an hour and then went back to my flat.

FENTON: Was Miss Brooks with you?

ROBIN: She came part of the way and then remembered she'd left her gloves at the hospital. She went back for them and then joined me later.

FENTON: At your mother's?

ROBIN: No, at my flat. I phoned mother at about half past nine and to my astonishment Mrs Walters, that's my housekeeper, told me she was out. She said Mardie had left and refused to say

78

where she was going. I waited until ten o'clock and then phoned again. She was still out so Linda and I went round to the house – it's in Montpelier Square – and waited there until a quarter past eleven. Then we decided to go down to the hospital: I don't quite know why, except that we were rather desperate by this stage and we just didn't know what to do. We were leaving the house when Inspector Austin arrived.

FENTON: I see. Let me get you some coffee. I'm sure you've had nothing this morning.

FENTON rises.

ROBIN follows him over to the table.

ROBIN: Fenton, do you think it's possible that my mother wasn't quite, well – herself?

FENTON: If you mean, do I think she was mentally unbalanced, then the answer is 'no'. She struck me as being a particularly sane type of woman.

ROBIN: Yes, I know, and I agree; but she was a little eccentric. Dash it all, you've got to admit that yourself. Look at all those notes she used to write.

FENTON: You can be eccentric without being mentally unbalanced.

ROBIN: Yes, but – well – (*Facing FENTON*) I'm quite sure that if my mother had been in her right senses she never would have gone to the Polygon Club.

FENTON: How do you know that she did go there?

ROBIN: But they found her there!

FENTON: (*Quietly*) Yes, I know that; but you misunderstand me. I mean – how do you know

	that she wasn't taken there after she was murdered?
ROBIN:	I hadn't thought of that. (*Slowly*) Of course, that would account for it, wouldn't it? Yes – she was murdered somewhere else, and then to divert suspicion – the murderer took her to the Polygon Club.
FENTON:	Well, it's a possibility. Here, drink this coffee.

FENTON hands ROBIN a cup of coffee.

ROBIN:	Thank you.

A moment's pause.

FENTON:	How's your fiancée taken this?
ROBIN:	She's taken it very well, considering. She was very fond of Mardie. It was Mardie who first introduced us.
FENTON:	I see.

The door bell rings.

FENTON:	Will you excuse me? I think that's Dr Sefton.

FENTON crosses the room and goes out into the hall.

He opens the front door.

INSPECTOR AUSTIN is in the doorway. His manner is distinctly officious.

AUSTIN:	Mr Fenton, I want to have a word with you. May I come in?
FENTON:	Yes, of course. Robin Terry's here.
AUSTIN:	(*Surprised*) Oh. How long has he been here?
FENTON:	About two or three minutes. Naturally, he's very upset.
AUSTIN:	Get rid of him.

They walk through into the drawing room.

AUSTIN:	Oh, good morning, Mr Terry.
ROBIN:	Oh, good morning, Inspector.
AUSTIN:	I want to talk to Mr Fenton. Will you excuse us?

ROBIN: Why – yes, of course. (*He hesitates*) Is there any news?

AUSTIN: No – not yet. (*He looks at FENTON*) But I think there might be – very soon.

FENTON: (*To ROBIN*) If you feel I can be of any help you can always find me here or at the hospital.

ROBIN: Thank you. Goodbye, Inspector.

AUSTIN: Goodbye, Mr Terry.

FENTON takes ROBIN TERRY through the alcove.

After TERRY has left FENTON returns to the drawing room.

FENTON: I'm afraid he's in a pretty bad way.

AUSTIN: He's not the only one.

FENTON: What d'ye mean?

AUSTIN: I'm in a pretty bad way myself this morning.

FENTON: Oh?

AUSTIN: I don't like being made a fool of!

FENTON: No one does, Inspector.

AUSTIN: And, you made a fool out of me, Mr Fenton.

FENTON: I did? When?

AUSTIN: Well, I suspect you started on the job the day Edward Schroder was murdered.

FENTON: I'm – afraid I don't follow you, Inspector?

AUSTIN: No? Well, I'll be more explicit. There's a report from Germany that Sir Oliver Peters arrived in East Berlin early on Tuesday morning.

FENTON: But they've been saying that sort of thing for the last five days! I tell you Peters is here in England. I operated on him! Good heavens, I thought I'd convinced you, Inspector.

AUSTIN: You nearly did, but not quite.

FENTON: What do you mean?

AUSTIN: I think your story about Peters was a deliberate lie to confuse the real issue.

FENTON: (*Annoyed*) Well, if Peters isn't the real issue, what is?

AUSTIN: (*Facing FENTON*) So far as I'm concerned the real issue is the murder of Edward Schroder and the murder of Mrs Beatrice Terry.

FENTON: Do you think I murdered Schroder?

AUSTIN: It's been established that the shot that killed Schroder was fired across the street, therefore you couldn't actually have fired it – but I think you know who did.

FENTON: And Mrs Terry?

AUSTIN: Supposing you tell me about Mrs Terry?

FENTON: (*Hesitantly*) There's nothing to tell: she was a patient of mine. I'd never set eyes on her until she was brought to the hospital. If you want to know about her why don't you ask her son?

AUSTIN: I've already done so. He told me about the picture. He said you made no comment about the Golden Valley.

FENTON: Of course I made no comment! I couldn't without telling him about Sir Oliver Peters. In any case, that's not strictly accurate. I was quite obviously surprised when he mentioned the Golden Valley, he must have noticed it.

AUSTIN: (*Casually*) Yes, he noticed it. (*He looks at FENTON for a moment*) What time did you say it was when you got home last night?

FENTON: About a quarter to eleven.

AUSTIN: You came straight here – from Oscar's?

FENTON: Yes.

AUSTIN: Mr Fenton, you remember when Dr Sefton was leaving, I helped him on with his overcoat.

FENTON: Yes.

AUSTIN: His coat was wet. It didn't start to rain until half past eleven.

FENTON: What are you suggesting?

AUSTIN: (*Quite simply*) Isn't it obvious? I'm suggesting that Dr Sefton was out in the rain.

FENTON: (*After a moment*) He – went down to the tobacconists. We ran out of cigarettes.

AUSTIN: (*A shade too polite*) What time was that?

FENTON: I suppose it must have been after half past eleven.

AUSTIN: Yes, I suppose it must have been.

There is an awkward silence.

FENTON: The shop was closed but – the proprietor's a friend of mine, if that's what you're thinking.

AUSTIN: (*Nodding; quietly*) That's what I was thinking. I was also thinking it's rather an unfortunate coincidence that your fingerprints were on the telephone at the Polygon Club.

FENTON: My fingerprints – but I – I can't understand that.

AUSTIN: No, I didn't think you would.

AUSTIN takes out his watch and looks at it.

AUSTIN: Mr Fenton, I have a reputation amongst my colleagues of being a little – what shall I say? – unorthodox. Take this morning for instance. I should have a colleague with me and I should of course issue a warning that anything you say will be taken down and may be used in evidence. However, I don't propose to do that – not yet.

FENTON: What do you mean?

AUSTIN: Think things over. Perhaps you were wrong about Sir Oliver Peters. Perhaps the man you operated on wasn't Peters after all. Perhaps you

83

can think of the real reason why Edward Schroder was murdered.

DR SEFTON enters through the alcove.

SEFTON: You know you're going to be burgled if you leave the door open all night. Oh, good morning, Inspector!

AUSTIN: (*A change of manner; quite bright*) Good morning, Dr Sefton!

SEFTON: (*To FENTON*) The door was open, Mark. So I thought –

FENTON: Yes, of course.

AUSTIN: Don't worry. I'll let myself out. Goodbye, doctor!

SEFTON: Goodbye, Inspector.

AUSTIN: (*To FENTON*) Goodbye, Mr Fenton. (*Pleasantly*) Think over what we've been talking about. (*To SEFTON*) Is it raining, doctor?

SEFTON: No, it's quite fine.

AUSTIN: Oh, splendid!

AUSTIN smiles and goes out.

A pause.

The front door closes.

SEFTON: What's happened?

FENTON: He knows about last night. He felt your overcoat; it was damp.

SEFTON: Well?

FENTON: It didn't start raining until half past eleven.

SEFTON: Oh – oh, I'm sorry, Mark.

FENTON: There's nothing for you to be sorry about. Would you like some coffee?

SEFTON: No, thank you. What else did he say?

FENTON: They found my fingerprints on the telephone at the Polygon Club. He thinks I murdered Mrs

84

	Terry and that I was mixed up in the Schroder murder.
SEFTON:	He thinks you murdered Mrs Terry?
FENTON:	Yes – at least that's the impression he gave me.
SEFTON:	But that's nonsense!
FENTON:	I know it's nonsense, but how can I prove it? I don't know what to do, Andrew. If I tell them the truth – they obviously won't believe, well – they don't believe that Peters has got anything to do with this business.
SEFTON:	But they've got to believe you! You've got to convince them once and for all that you did see Peters!
FENTON:	Yes, but how? How? There's only one way I'll ever convince them.
SEFTON:	You mean – find Peters?
FENTON:	Yes.
SEFTON:	(*Almost a joke*) All right, old boy. Then we'll have to find him!

The telephone starts ringing.

SEFTON: Ten to one it's Gillespie.

FENTON lifts the receiver.

FENTON: (*On the phone*) Hello? … Yes … Yes, speaking … (*Surprised*) Oh, good morning. (*He puts his hand over the receiver; to SEFTON*) It's that girl – Linda Brooks. (*On the phone*) Yes … Yes, of course … I will … Well, why don't you come to the hospital? … I see … Well – where would you suggest? … You mean the one in Piccadilly? … Yes, of course I know it … All right, four o'clock this afternoon … Yes, I'll be there … No … No, all right, Miss Brooks. Goodbye!

FENTON replaces the receiver.

SEFTON: What did she want?

FENTON: She said she wanted to see me and that it was
            urgent. It sounded urgent too, the way she
            spoke.

SEFTON: Do you think she knows anything about Mrs
            Terry?

FENTON: I think Miss Brooks knows a great deal about a
            great many things. (*A tiny pause: quietly*)
            Andrew –

SEFTON: Yes?

FENTON: Seriously – you don't really think we could
            find Sir Oliver Peters?

SEFTON: Well – we could try.

CUT TO: A Café in Piccadilly.

*The café has bench style seating. A high-backed partition
separates the tables from each other.*

LINDA BROOKS is sitting facing the table.

FENTON's hat is on the seat by her side.

FENTON enters carrying two cups of tea.

*He places the cups on the table, moves his hat to one side,
and sits down.*

LINDA: Thank you.

FENTON: I don't know whether you take sugar or not?

LINDA: It really doesn't matter.

FENTON drinks his tea; he looks at LINDA as he drinks.

FENTON: Well, Miss Brooks?

LINDA: (*Hesitantly*) You know about – Mrs Terry?

FENTON: Yes, I know. Is that why you wanted to see me?

LINDA: No, it isn't really anything to do with Mrs
            Terry. I … (*She looks about her, not wishing to
            be overheard*) Sir Oliver Peters is ill …
            desperately ill … we don't know what to do …

FENTON: What's happened?

86

LINDA:	He seemed to take a turn for the worse yesterday. He was in a coma for most of the morning.
FENTON:	Did you get a doctor?
LINDA:	No, of course we didn't.
FENTON:	Then I suggest that you get one.
LINDA:	But don't you understand …
FENTON:	I understand this, Miss Brooks. You and your delightful friends abducted Sir Oliver and soon after he was taken ill you had to send for a surgeon. Now I don't know what you intend to do with Peters, but I warn you – he's a sick man – a very sick man – and if he doesn't receive medical attention …
LINDA:	(*Interrupting FENTON*) Believe me, it isn't a question of what I decide. If I had my way I should release Sir Oliver immediately, but …
FENTON:	But what? You know where Peters is. All you've got to do is go straight to Scotland Yard and tell them.
LINDA:	And what do you think would happen if I did?
FENTON:	What would happen?
LINDA:	You saw what happened to Edward Schroder …
FENTON:	(*Watching LINDA*) Was Schroder a friend of yours?
LINDA:	(*Distressed*) Yes, he was.

A tiny pause.

FENTON:	Docs your fiancé – Robin Terry – know that you are mixed up in this business?
LINDA:	No …
FENTON:	Are you sure?
LINDA:	Quite sure. He doesn't know anything about Edward – or Peters – or anything …

FENTON: And what about Mrs Terry – did she know? Is that why she was murdered?

LINDA: I don't know. Mr Fenton, I phoned you this morning because Wade – he's the man who was in the ambulance the night you were picked up …

FENTON: Yes, I remember Mr Wade.

LINDA: Well – Wade would like you to see Peters again.

FENTON: Would he? (*Thoughtfully*) Would he, now?

FENTON looks at his cup and sips his tea.

FENTON: All right, Miss Brooks. I'll take a look at Peters – on one condition.

LINDA: What's that?

FENTON: Go back to Mr Wade and tell him that my fee will be five hundred pounds – payable in one pound notes.

LINDA: Do you really mean …

FENTON: If Wade is prepared to pay me five hundred pounds I'll look after Peters for him – for a time at any rate. If he isn't, that's just too bad.

LINDA: You're not serious.

FENTON: On the contrary, I'm perfectly serious, Miss Brooks.

LINDA rises.

LINDA: (*Looking down at FENTON*) You know Hammersmith – King's Theatre?

FENTON: Yes, of course.

LINDA: A car will pick you up there this evening, five o'clock.

FENTON: I'll be there.

FENTON looks up at LINDA and gives a little smile.

FENTON: Don't forget – five hundred pounds, in one pound notes.

LINDA looks down at FENTON for a moment, then turns and goes.

FENTON sits looking after her.

After a little while he rises, picks up his hat, and leaves the table.

ROBIN TERRY is sitting at the table on the other side of the partition, a cup of tea in front of him, an illustrated magazine open on the table.

He is smiling.

CUT TO: Hammersmith. Night.

FENTON is walking up and down on the pavement near Hammersmith Underground Station. He is looking about him; waiting for the car.

He wears an overcoat, homburg hat and carries his bag.

A car draws up to the pavement near FENTON.

It is driven by LINDA.

MORGAN jumps out of the car and touches FENTON on the sleeve.

FENTON hesitates, then recognises LINDA at the driving wheel; he follows MORGAN into the car.

The car drives away.

As the car drives away from the kerb the camera pans across the pavement to the doorway of a shop.

COLONEL WYMAN is in the doorway, leaning nonchalantly against the side window, smoking a cigarette. He watches the car depart.

CUT TO: A Room In A Country House (as in Episode 1)

The room is as described in Episode 1 – in which FENTON performed the operation on SIR OLIVER PETERS.

There is a window; two doors – one leading from the hall and another into a corridor – several chairs, a standard lamp, a mirror on the wall, etc.

SIR OLIVER PETERS is in bed in a corner of the room; the young NURSE – the girl in the ambulance in Episode 1 – is giving Sir Oliver a drink of water from a medicine glass.

WADE is standing back closing the curtains.

There is the sound of a car and a beam of light flashes across the window.

The car stops; the lights are switched off.

WADE: Here they are! And not before time!

NURSE: What time is it?

WADE: It must be getting on for one o'clock. (*He takes out his watch*) It's nearly a quarter past.

NURSE: What time were they supposed to pick him up?

WADE: Half past ten. That's about right, isn't it? Half past ten to half past eleven – half past twelve … About two and a half hours … That's about right … (*He looks down at PETERS*) By the Lord Harry, he doesn't look too good, does he?

NURSE: No, but he seems better than he did …

WADE: I think perhaps you'd better fetch some towels – an' some hot water.

NURSE: Yes – it'll take time.

WADE: Do what you can.

The NURSE goes out through the door into the corridor.

PETERS looks in great pain.

WADE: (*To PETERS*) How are you feeling? Have you still got the pain?

PETERS nods his head to WADE.

WADE: Well, don't worry, there's a doctor coming. He'll look after you. We don't want you to die, you know – don't get that idea into your head.

FENTON enters followed by LINDA and MORGAN.

He is blindfolded and as he enters the room MORGAN passes behind him and unties the handkerchief.

The light blinds FENTON: he covers his eyes with his hands.

WADE: Good evening, Mr Fenton. (*To MORGAN*) All right?

MORGAN: Yes – perfect.

WADE: No trouble?

MORGAN: No.

WADE: Where's the car – still in the front?

MORGAN: Yes.

WADE: Take it round to the back, but don't put it away.

MORGAN: Yes, all right. (*He hesitates*) How are things at this end? You haven't heard, I suppose?

WADE: Of course not, it's too early.

MORGAN looks at FENTON, then goes out the main door.

WADE crosses to FENTON.

WADE: Well, Mr Fenton?

FENTON: You got my message?

WADE: (*Quite friendly*) The money's here – don't worry, you'll have it before you go. I promise you, you'll have the money.

FENTON looks at WADE, then crosses to the bed.

He stares down at PETERS and feels his pulse.

LINDA: (*Quietly; to WADE*) Where's Kay – upstairs?

WADE nods: he is watching FENTON.

LINDA goes out into the corridor.

WADE crosses to the bed.

FENTON suddenly puts his bag down on a nearby chair and takes off his hat and coat.

WADE takes the hat and coat and stands watching FENTON.

FENTON stoops down and examines PETERS and feels his pulse again.

A pause.

WADE: Well?

91

FENTON: The pulse is very weak and irregular.

WADE: And what does that mean?

FENTON: It means he should have been sent to a hospital twenty-four hours ago. I doubt very much whether there's anything I can do.

WADE: (*Taking hold of FENTON's arm; angrily*) What do you mean – you doubt whether there's anything you can do?

FENTON: (*Releasing his arm; with authority*) Get me some water – cold water – straight away …

WADE indicates a glass of drinking water on a side table.

WADE: There's some on the side there …

FENTON rolls up his sleeves.

FENTON: Do you want me to help this man, or don't you?

WADE: Yes, of course!

FENTON: Then do as I say! Get me some cold water – fresh water – straight away!

WADE watches FENTON; hesitates; then puts FENTON's hat and coat down and goes out through the door into the corridor.

The moment WADE has departed FENTON turns away from the bed and opens his bag and takes out a small Leica camera: he looks up just in case WADE should return unexpectedly.

FENTON adjusts the camera, stands facing the bed, raises the camera to his right eye, and takes a photograph of PETERS.

Immediately he has taken the photograph he returns the camera to the bag.

He is stooping over the bag as WADE returns with a jug of water.

FENTON: Put it on the table over there.

FENTON takes the water from WADE and puts it on the table under the mirror on the wall.

The NURSE enters carrying several towels and a bowl of hot water. She places it on the table.

FENTON slowly prepares an injection.

Having prepared the syringe he inserts it into the top of a glass bottle.

He watches the preparation for a moment and then casually raises his head and looks in the mirror.

His expression suddenly changes, the syringe falls from his hand.

Through the mirror FENTON can see DR SEFTON entering the room.

He is alone and is not blindfolded.

END OF EPISODE THREE

EPISODE FOUR

GIDA

OPEN TO: The Drawing Room in the Country House

FENTON slowly prepares an injection.

Having prepared the syringe he inserts it into the top of a glass bottle.

He watches the preparation for a moment and then casually raises his head and looks in the mirror.

His expression suddenly changes, the syringe falls from his hand.

Through the mirror FENTON can see DR SEFTON entering the room.

He is alone and is not blindfolded.

FENTON suddenly turns and faces the door.

HARRISON enters the room behind SEFTON; he is carrying a revolver and a handkerchief.

The revolver is pointed at SEFTON.

WADE and the NURSE are obviously surprised by SEFTON's entrance.

FENTON stares at SEFTON but doesn't speak or show any sign of recognition.

WADE: What happened?

HARRISON: (*Indicating SEFTON*) He was tailing the car! We did what you said … waited about five minutes and then followed the car. (*He nods towards SEFTON*) This fellow was tailing them. We had to pick him up, Wade, otherwise he'd have found this place.

WADE: Did you blindfold him?

HARRISON holds up the handkerchief.

HARRISON: Yes, of course.

WADE: (*Turns towards SEFTON*) Who is he?

HARRISON: I don't know.

WADE: Have you seen him before?

HARRISON: No.

97

WADE: Is he one of Gida's men?

HARRISON shrugs.

WADE: All right, Harrison. (*To SEFTON*) What's your name?

SEFTON doesn't reply.

WADE: Are you from Gida?

SEFTON still doesn't answer.

WADE: You heard what I said – are you one of Gida's men?

SEFTON: I don't know what you're talking about! I've never heard of anyone called Gida!

WADE: No?

WADE takes the revolver from HARRISON and advances towards SEFTON.

WADE: Well, who are you? (*Watching SEFTON*) Are you the police?

SEFTON: No.

WADE: You're not exactly co-operative. (*He raises the revolver*) I'll give you five seconds to tell me who you are and where you've come from.

FENTON: (*Quietly*) His name's Sefton – Dr Sefton. He's a friend of mine. I told him to tail the car in case, well – in case there was any funny business and I didn't get the money.

WADE: (*Looks at FENTON then back at SEFTON*) Dr Sefton, you say?

FENTON: Yes.

WADE: (*To SEFTON*) You say you've never heard of Gida?

SEFTON: I've already told you I haven't.

WADE: Are you both at the same hospital?

SEFTON: Yes.

WADE: (*To the NURSE*) Tell Linda I want her – she's upstairs.

NURSE: (*Puzzled*) Why do you want Linda?

WADE: (*Angry*) Don't argue! Fetch her!

The NURSE crosses and goes out into the corridor.

WADE: (*To HARRISON*) What did you use – the van?

HARRISON: Yes.

WADE: Put it in the garage.

HARRISON: O.K.

HARRISON goes out.

FENTON and SEFTON cross to the bed.

SEFTON looks down at PETERS and feels his pulse.

WADE is watching SEFTON.

FENTON: (*To SEFTON*) He's in a pretty bad way, I'm afraid. He looks to me as if he's developed an ileus.

SEFTON: (*Nodding*) Yes.

FENTON: I'm giving him a penicillin injection.

SEFTON: (*Nods; quietly*) Did you bring any plasma or saline?

FENTON: No.

SEFTON: I doubt very much whether penicillin will have any effect. What he needs are chlorides badly and fluids of course.

FENTON: Yes.

LINDA enters.

She immediately recognises SEFTON.

WADE: (*To LINDA*) Have you seen this man before?

LINDA: (*Surprised*) Yes, he's a doctor at St Mathew's Hospital. I think his name is Sefton ...

WADE: (*Relieved*) All right.

FENTON finishes the preparation for the penicillin.

LINDA: (*To WADE*) How did he get here?

WADE: He was tailing Fenton. Harrison picked him up.

FENTON is holding the syringe up ready for the injection.

SEFTON is examining PETERS.

The telephone rings.

WADE: (*Stopping LINDA*) I'll take it!

WADE looks towards the bed as he crosses the room.

SEFTON watches WADE cross towards the telephone.

WADE lifts the receiver but stands for a moment watching FENTON who is about to give PETERS the injection.

FENTON stoops down ready to plunge the needle into PETERS.

WADE: (*On the phone*) Hello? ... Oh, it's you ... Yes
          ... (*He watches FENTON and SEFTON*) Yes,
          he's here now ... No, not yet ... There's
          another man with him – a Dr Sefton ... No, he
          was tailing the car ... Harrison picked him up
          ... No, it's all right, there's nothing to worry
          about ... Of course, we took all the usual
          precautions ... (*He listens*)

A pause.

FENTON, curious about the telephone call, is watching WADE.

He has given PETERS the injection.

WADE: (*On the phone*) ... Is there any news? ...
          (*Irritated*) It's no good playing in with Gida –
          we're not going to get anything out of Gida
          except a packet of trouble ... Yes, all right.

WADE replaces the receiver.

WADE crosses the room and joins FENTON and SEFTON at the bed.

SEFTON has just completed a more detailed examination of PETERS.

He looks serious.

SEFTON: (*To WADE*) You've got to get this man to a
          hospital.

WADE: (*Smiling*) Have we now?

100

FENTON: This isn't a joke. If you don't get him to a hospital, Dr Sefton and I won't be responsible for the consequences.

WADE: Won't you now? (*Raising his voice*) Why the devil do you think we brought you here? You operated on him, didn't you? You know what's the matter with the man …

FENTON: We do.

WADE: Well, I don't care what you do or how you do it, but get him on his feet.

LINDA: (*Quietly, to FENTON*) What is the matter with him?

FENTON looks at SEFTON.

SEFTON: (*After a moment*) Mr Fenton operated for a volvulus. Unfortunately, Sir Oliver is still suffering from a temporary intestinal paralysis.

LINDA: What would you do if he was in hospital?

SEFTON: We should probably give him an intravenous of saline and glucose, and of course chloramphenicol.

WADE: Well, why can't you give it to him now?

FENTON: For the simple reason that we haven't got it.

WADE: Then get it!

FENTON: He's got to be moved.

WADE: That's impossible!

LINDA: (*Interrupting WADE*) Wait a minute! (*To FENTON*) This drug – is it difficult to get?

SEFTON: It's not easy.

WADE: But you can get it?

SEFTON: (*Hesitating*) Yes.

WADE: Supposing he doesn't have these drugs?

SEFTON: Then the chances are that he'll die.

WADE: All right. (*To LINDA*) Tell Morgan I want to see him.

101

LINDA goes out.
FENTON looks at SEFTON.
WADE crosses to the desk, opens a drawer and takes out several packets of pound notes.
He returns to the table.

WADE: Here's the money. Five hundred pounds – one pound notes. You can count it if you like.

FENTON: (*After a moment; taking the money*) I'll take your word for it.

FENTON crosses and puts the money in his bag.

WADE: (*With authority*) Now I'll tell you what I want you to do. Go back to Town and get the stuff you've been talking about.

FENTON: (*Interrupting WADE*) You can't just go into a shop and buy it like a bar of soap. It's very difficult stuff to get hold of. I'll do my best, but …

WADE: You'll do more than your best. You'll get it! (*A moment; quietly*) When you've got the stuff, take it back to your flat and wait. Someone will phone you and make arrangements to bring you down here.

FENTON: (*After a moment*) And supposing I don't get it?

WADE: What do you mean?

FENTON: Supposing I double-cross you and go to Scotland Yard?

WADE: You won't.

FENTON: Why not?

WADE: (*Smiling*) Because in the first place even if you did go to the Yard they wouldn't believe you. And in the second place, if you were stupid enough to double-cross us it would be just too bad – for Dr Sefton.

SEFTON: What do you mean?

102

WADE: (*Smiling*) You didn't imagine that Dr Sefton was going back to Town, did you now?

SEFTON: (*Angrily*) Of course I'm going back to Town.

WADE: Oh, no! You're staying here, Dr Sefton. (*He smiles*) With you here Mr Fenton is bound to behave himself. (*To FENTON*) You wouldn't like anything to happen to him, now, would you, Mr Fenton?

FENTON: Now look, Wade – let's be sensible about this. If you keep Sefton here they'll miss him at the hospital and …

WADE: (*Amused*) They've missed Sir Oliver Peters at the Foreign Office, but they still haven't found him. Don't argue the point. Sefton stays!

FENTON looks at SEFTON who slowly nods his head.

FENTON: All right, Wade. He stays.

MORGAN enters.

MORGAN: Did you want me?

WADE: You're taking Mr Fenton back to Town.

MORGAN: What – tonight?

WADE: Tonight.

MORGAN: What car?

WADE: Take the van.

MORGAN: All right.

FENTON: (*Hesitating*) There's just one point.

WADE: Yes?

FENTON: Supposing Peters gets better – gets on his feet again, I mean. What are you going to do with him?

WADE: Isn't that obvious? Peters is a very important man. He knows more about Western Defence than any other diplomat.

FENTON: You still haven't answered my question.

WADE: We intend to hand him over, Mr Fenton.

103

FENTON:	You mean – to the Russians?
WADE:	Not necessarily. It all depends.
FENTON:	(*Puzzled*) On what?
WADE:	(*Smiling*) On the price, Mr Fenton – on the price.

CUT TO: The Main Entrance of Scotland Yard.

A taxi drives up and FENTON jumps out, tells the driver to wait for him, and enters the building.

He is wearing a hat and coat and carries his bag.

CUT TO: INSPECTOR AUSTIN's Office at Scotland Yard.

DETECTIVE INSPECTOR AUSTIN is sitting in a swivel chair behind his desk.

He is writing a report.

There is a large Metropolitan area map on one of the walls.

A uniformed SERGEANT enters and places a folder on the desk.

The telephone rings and AUSTIN lifts the receiver.

The SERGEANT stands by the desk.

AUSTIN:	(*On the phone*) Hello? … Yes … Who? … Yes, very well … Ask him to come up …

AUSTIN replaces the receiver.

SERGEANT:	(*Indicating the folder*) A report on the Kimford case, sir, and the Fenton warrant.
AUSTIN:	Thank you, Sergeant. Mr Fenton's on his way up. I'll see him immediately.
SERGEANT:	Yes, sir.

The SERGEANT leaves.

AUSTIN picks up the folder and opens it.

He reads one of the documents; pushes the folder on one side and picks up the telephone.

AUSTIN: (*On the phone*) I don't want to be disturbed.
               (*He looks at his watch*) Don't put any calls
               through to this office until after eleven
               o'clock.

AUSTIN replaces the receiver.

The SERGEANT re-enters followed by MARK FENTON.

SERGEANT: Mr Fenton, sir.

AUSTIN: Good morning, Mr Fenton.

The SERGEANT exits.

*FENTON doesn't reply to AUSTIN but stands by the chair
facing the desk.*

AUSTIN: (*Indicating the chair*) Sit down.

FENTON sits.

A pause.

AUSTIN: Well? What can I do for you?

*FENTON looks at AUSTIN; he opens his bag and takes out
the bank notes which were given him by WADE.*

FENTON: You can take care of these.

AUSTIN: (*Puzzled*) What is it?

FENTON throws the notes onto the desk.

FENTON: It's five hundred pounds.

AUSTIN: Five hundred pounds!

FENTON: Yes – in one pound notes. (*Smiling*) It's the
            largest fee I've earned, Inspector – so take
            care of it.

AUSTIN: (*Angrily*) Is this a joke?

FENTON: If it is, the joke's on you – for a change.

AUSTIN: What do you mean? Where did you get this
               money?

FENTON: A Mr Wade gave it to me – for services
            rendered.

AUSTIN: Wade? (*Surprised*) The Irishman: the man
               you said was with Sir Oliver Peters?

FENTON: That's right, Inspector.

105

AUSTIN: Fenton, what's this all about?

FENTON: You didn't believe my story about Peters, did you? You thought I was lying!

AUSTIN: You were lying! You said you'd never been to the Polygon Club. You said you knew nothing about Mrs Terry.

FENTON: (*Leaning forward*) I'm not talking about the Polygon Club or Mrs Terry, I'm talking about Sir Oliver Peters.

A moment.

AUSTIN: Well?

FENTON: Why do you think Wade gave me the five hundred pounds?

AUSTIN: I haven't the slightest idea.

FENTON: Well, I'll tell you why, Inspector. He gave it to me because that was the only condition under which I was prepared to make a further examination of Sir Oliver Peters.

AUSTIN: Are you trying to tell me that you've seen Peters – again?

FENTON: Yes, I saw him last night. He was very ill – that's why Wade sent for me.

AUSTIN rises and goes to the window.

He comes back to his desk.

AUSTIN: I don't know whether you're a fool or extremely shrewd.

FENTON: I'm neither, Inspector. I just want to convince you, once and for all, that I was telling you the truth about Sir Oliver Peters.

AUSTIN: Look, forgetting Peters for the moment. Can you explain why you lied to me? Can you explain why you went to the Polygon Club in the first place?

FENTON: I can.

106

AUSTIN: (*Angrily*) Then why don't you?

FENTON: I've told you why.

AUSTIN: You mean you intend to hold out on me until I accept the Peters story?

FENTON: I've got to, Inspector, because if you don't accept the Peters story you'll never accept my version of what happened the night Mrs Terry was murdered.

AUSTIN: M'm.

AUSTIN turns and picks up some of the bank notes.

AUSTIN: Why did you insist on the money?

FENTON: I wanted Wade to think that I was playing in with them. I thought if I gave him the impression that I needed money he might be tempted to look on me as one of themselves.

AUSTIN: Did he?

FENTON: No.

AUSTIN: (*A slight change of manner*) How do I know that Wade gave you this money?

FENTON: You don't, you've just got to accept my word for it.

AUSTIN hesitates; he is not sure whether to believe FENTON or not.

FENTON: You're not sure, are you, Inspector?

AUSTIN: Look, Mr Fenton – I'd like to believe you! I want to believe you! But just because you come along here with five hundred pounds …

FENTON: (*Smiling*) … and the photograph.

AUSTIN: What photograph?

FENTON: (*Unable to conceal a note of triumph*) Oh, didn't I show you the photograph, Inspector?

FENTON takes a photograph out of his inside pocket and holds it up so that AUSTIN can see it.

The INSPECTOR takes the photo out of FENTON's hand.

AUSTIN: It's Peters!

FENTON: Yes.

AUSTIN: But – when was this taken?

FENTON: Last night. (*Leaning towards AUSTIN; eager to convince*) I took a camera with me and managed to get Wade out of the room. While he was out I took the photograph.

AUSTIN: Good Lord!

AUSTIN stares at the photograph, walks up and down and then suddenly turns and looks down at FENTON.

AUSTIN: I believe you, Fenton!

AUSTIN looks at the photograph.

AUSTIN: It's fantastic, but I believe you!

AUSTIN returns to the desk and picks up the phone.

AUSTIN: (*On the phone*) Tell Inspector Lester I want him in my office straight away … Yes, it's urgent!

AUSTIN replaces the receiver.

AUSTIN: Now, what happened the night Mrs Terry was murdered? Why the devil did you go to the Polygon Club?

CUT TO: The Central Telephone Exchange.

Telephone girls are busy at work.

1st GIRL: I'm sorry, sir, Inspector Austin can't be disturbed … No, I'm sorry, sir … Mr Murray? … Yes, I'll put you through.

2nd GIRL: Inspector Austin's in conference at present … No, I'm sorry, sir, we can't put you through … Yes, all right, sir.

3rd GIRL: I'm afraid there's no reply from Inspector Austin's office … Yes, I've kept ringing … Sorry, sir.

CUT TO: AUSTIN's Office.

AUSTIN is sitting in his chair behind the desk, leaning forward, listening to FENTON.

INSPECTOR LESTER is standing near the desk, looking down at FENTON.

FENTON: … They blindfolded me and brought me back to Town. It was about half past one when I arrived at my flat.

AUSTIN: How long did the journey take?

FENTON: I should say between two and a half and three hours.

AUSTIN: In other words – you reckon the house is about eighty or ninety miles out of Town?

FENTON: (*Hesitating*) Yes.

LESTER: (*To AUSTIN*) Well, that ties up with the Golden Valley, doesn't it? Cirencester's about ninety.

AUSTIN: Yes, but according to Wyman the Special Branch people have been over every inch of that district.

FENTON: (*Thoughtfully*) You know, it's a curious thing – although the journey took at least two and a half hours I had the feeling that they were killing time. I've got a hunch that the house isn't so far out of Town, that they've been making a deliberate detour to put me off.

LESTER: Then why did Sir Oliver make a reference to the Golden Valley? He must have thought he was in the Cotswolds otherwise he wouldn't have mentioned it.

FENTON: Yes, that's true.

AUSTIN: Mr Fenton, you say that Wade mentioned a man called Gida?

FENTON: Yes. As soon as he saw Andrew – Dr Sefton –
           he accused him of being one of Gida's men. I
           don't know what he meant.

FENTON rises.

AUSTIN: Had you heard that name – Gida – before?

FENTON: No, never.

AUSTIN: What about the telephone call Wade received –
           have you any idea who it was?

FENTON: No, but Wade said – "We've taken all the usual
           precautions". I'm sure he wasn't just referring
           to the fact that I was blindfolded.

AUSTIN: You think he was referring to the journey?

FENTON: Yes.

AUSTIN: M'm.

AUSTIN holds out his hand.

AUSTIN: Well, thank you, Mr Fenton. Now don't forget
           – get in touch with us the moment you hear
           from them. Don't ring the Yard, ring the
           number I gave you. The Welbeck number.

FENTON: Yes, all right, but I hope you'll be careful,
           Inspector, because Dr Sefton's a friend of mine
           and I wouldn't like to think that anything was
           going to happen to him …

AUSTIN: Don't worry, we understand the position
           perfectly. That's why I want you to ring that
           number instead of the Yard.

AUSTIN crosses to the door.

AUSTIN: We shan't take any risks as far as Dr Sefton's
           concerned – on the other hand, we've got to
           find Peters!

AUSTIN opens the door.

FENTON: Yes, of course. Goodbye, Inspector.

LESTER: Goodbye, Mr Fenton.

FENTON goes out with INSPECTOR AUSTIN.

LESTER picks up one of the bank notes off the desk; he holds it up to the light, examines it and feels it with his fingers.

AUSTIN returns.

LESTER: (*Turning*) Well – these look genuine enough.

AUSTIN: (*Briskly; crossing to his desk*) Yes – and so's that story of his.

AUSTIN lifts the telephone receiver.

AUSTIN: (*On the phone*) Get me Colonel Wyman – Department M – Extension 3 … Ring me back.

AUSTIN replaces the receiver. He looks thoughtful.

LESTER: Did Wyman tell you about his visit to the Polygon Club?

AUSTIN: No; I thought he was in the Cotswolds.

LESTER: If Fenton's telling the truth it looks as if Wyman was the first to see Mrs Terry – after she was murdered, I mean.

AUSTIN: Yes. Why didn't he tell us? These Special Branch people! They seem to think they're a law unto themselves!

LESTER: They never tell anybody anything, old boy – not if they can help it.

AUSTIN: How long have you known Wyman?

LESTER: About eighteen months. We used to meet down at Birchington. He has a bungalow down there.

AUSTIN: (*Faintly on his dignity*) Birchington? That's near Margate, isn't it?

LESTER: Yes.

AUSTIN: Really.

LESTER: He was with the Foreign Office to start with, you know.

AUSTIN: It's a pity he didn't stay with them.

LESTER: Oh, I don't know. I rather like Wyman.

AUSTIN: M'm.

111

LESTER: He's a curious bird, though. (*Smiling*) Do you
           know what he does as a hobby?

AUSTIN: No?

LESTER: He entertains youngsters. He's a ventriloquist;
           he's got an act – you know, a dummy and
           everything. (*Amused*) The dummy's dressed up
           as a policeman – he's darn clever!

LESTER laughs.

AUSTIN gives him a look: he is not amused.

CUT TO: FENTON's Office at St Mathew's Hospital.

*FENTON is sitting at his desk examining a slide through a
microscope.*

There are several X-rays on the desk.

SISTER ROGERS enters; she is carrying a folder.

FENTON looks up.

FENTON: Did Dr Gillespie say anything about Miss
           Cartwright?

SISTER: I've just been talking to him about her. He's
           arranged for Sir Gilbert to see her.

SISTER ROGERS looks at the papers in the folder.

SISTER: Tuesday afternoon – four o'clock.

SISTER ROGERS places the folder on the desk.

FENTON opens his diary.

FENTON: I see I've got an appointment at three …

SISTER: (*Looking at the diary*) Yes, a Mr Christie – he
           telephoned this morning while you were out.
           He's a patient of Dr Melton's.

FENTON: Oh, what is it? Do you know?

SISTER: I've put the details in your diary.

FENTON: Thank you, Sister. (*Casually*) Did anyone else
           call?

SISTER: No … (*Suddenly*) Oh, yes, Mr Terry. He said
            he wanted to see you and I suggested two-
            thirty.

FENTON looks at his watch.

FENTON: It's after that now.

SISTER: He's probably forgotten all about it. The poor
            man's in a dreadful state; it'll surprise me if he
            doesn't have a breakdown.

FENTON: Yes.

SISTER: I feel awfully sorry for him. He seemed so
            devoted to his mother.

FENTON: Yes … (*He turns towards his microscope*) I
            suppose the Matron told you about Dr Sefton?

SISTER ROGERS nods.

SISTER: Is it serious?

FENTON: No, it's just a cold. A real snorter!

SISTER: Well, thank goodness he's got the common
            sense to stay away.

There is a knock on the door.

SISTER ROGERS crosses to the door and opens it.

*ROBIN TERRY is standing there; he looks worried and
distinctly on edge.*

SISTER: Good afternoon, Mr Terry!

ROBIN: Hello, Sister.

FENTON rises.

FENTON: Come in, Terry!

ROBIN TERRY enters.

SISTER ROGERS goes out, closing the door behind her.

ROBIN: You did ask me to call and see you if … I
            wasn't feeling too good.

FENTON: Yes, of course.

ROBIN: I haven't been sleeping well lately – as a matter
            of fact, I haven't been sleeping at all. I thought

113

if you could give me something it ... might ... help.

FENTON: Yes, but why don't you go away for a little while? Go abroad – a complete change of environment.

ROBIN: I've thought about it, but – I don't know. I wouldn't mind if I could get some sleep. Actually, I've been commissioned to paint two pictures, but, somehow – I just don't feel capable of anything.

FENTON: I'll give you a prescription for some sleeping tablets. Take two – last thing at night.

FENTON writes on a pad on his desk.

FENTON: You'll get some sleep anyway.

ROBIN: Well, that'll be something, thank goodness!

FENTON finishes writing the prescription.

FENTON: (*Quietly; not looking up*) How's your fiancée, Mr Terry?

ROBIN: (*Puzzled; worried*) I don't know. That's another thing that's worrying me. I haven't seen Linda – for two days. I keep ringing her flat but – there's no reply. You know, since my mother died Linda's been rather strange. She was always a very good friend of Mardie's – they went about quite a lot together – but she refuses to discuss Mardie, or the murder, or anything to do with this affair.

FENTON: Well, that's understandable, surely? People react to things in different ways.

ROBIN: (*Thoughtfully*) Yes ... Yes, I suppose they do ...

The door opens and SISTER ROGERS enters.

SISTER: (*To FENTON*) Mr Christie's arrived.

FENTON: Yes, all right, Sister. Mr Terry's just leaving.

FENTON gives ROBIN TERRY the prescription.

FENTON: Here's your prescription. Take two tablets last thing at night; not more than two.

ROBIN: Thank you.

They shake hands.

ROBIN: I'm sorry to have made such a nuisance of myself.

FENTON: Nonsense!

ROBIN TERRY goes out with SISTER ROGERS.

FENTON returns to the desk and consults his diary.

After a moment SISTER ROGERS returns with MICHAEL CHRISTIE. He is a rather pleasant man in his thirties.

FENTON and CHRISTIE shake hands.

FENTON: Mr Christie …

CHRISTIE: Yes … Good afternoon, Mr Fenton.

FENTON indicates the chair near the desk.

FENTON: Sit down. I'll be with you in a moment. (*To SISTER ROGERS*) Sister, would you tell the girl on the switchboard to put my calls through – she sometimes doesn't when I've got private patients.

SISTER: (*A shade surprised*) You want the calls put through?

FENTON: Yes, please.

SISTER ROGERS goes out.

FENTON: (*Turning towards CHRISTIE*) Now, Mr Christie.

FENTON returns to his desk and looks down at his diary.

FENTON: I understand you're a patient of Dr Sefton's.

CHRISTIE: Yes. Dr Melton seems to think I've got a slipped disc but – well, I'm not so sure.

FENTON: (*Smiling*) What makes you – not so sure?

CHRISTIE: Well, I was in Nice about six weeks ago and I had a pretty bad attack. The doctor made me

115

have an X-ray – and the X-rays didn't show anything.

FENTON: I see. Well, naturally, Mr Christie, I don't quite know why you came to see me, because I'm a surgeon. If it is a slipped disc I might of course come into the picture at a later date, but at the moment I really think you ought to see Dr Gillespie.

CHRISTIE: Well, I'll see Dr Gillespie if you want me to, of course – but, it was really you I wanted to see, Dr Fenton.

FENTON: Did Dr Melton tell you to come and see me?

CHRISTIE: Oh, no. Your name was mentioned to me about two months ago – by a mutual friend.

FENTON: Indeed?

CHRISTIE: Yes. (*Quietly*) Dr Schroder.

FENTON: (*Surprised*) Schroder?

CHRISTIE: (*Smiling*) Yes, don't tell me you've forgotten Edward Schroder. He was murdered – in your flat, if I remember rightly.

FENTON: (*After a moment; quietly*) Who are you? What do you want?

CHRISTIE: (*He looks towards the door to make certain it is closed; his manner changes; he is alert, excited*) My name's Christie – Michael Christie. I didn't lie about my name, but I'm a reporter on The Evening Post. I started to investigate the Schroder case and discovered that you were mixed up in it. I thought if I could have a private talk with you …

FENTON: (*Annoyed*) There's nothing I can tell you about the Schroder murder that you don't already know!

CHRISTIE: But you don't know what I know, Mr Fenton.

116

FENTON: (*Angrily; lifting the telephone receiver*) I know that you got in here under false pretences, and I'm going to have the Medical Superintendent …

CHRISTIE: (*Putting his hand on FENTON's*) One moment! Please!

FENTON hesitates then replaces the receiver.

FENTON: Well?

CHRISTIE: I'm sorry about the slipped disc nonsense but – I had to see you.

FENTON: Why?

CHRISTIE: Can't we sit down?

FENTON: No we can't. Say what you've got to say and then get out!

CHRISTIE: I'm convinced that the Schroder murder wasn't just a routine murder case. I may be wrong about this – you may think I'm crazy – but I think the Schroder murder was tied up in some way with the disappearance of Sir Oliver Peters.

FENTON: (*After a moment; obviously impressed*) I still don't see why you want to talk to me.

CHRISTIE: Schroder was found in your flat.

FENTON: Yes; he came to see me.

CHRISTIE: Why?

FENTON: I've already explained why to Scotland Yard.

CHRISTIE: (*Earnestly*) Look, Mr Fenton – I know certain things about this business, things which even Scotland Yard don't know. I've almost got the complete story, almost but not quite – there are just one or two pieces missing. When I get those pieces I'll hit Fleet Street with the biggest crime story they've had in years.

117

FENTON: You still haven't answered my question. Why have you come to see me?

CHRISTIE: (*Facing FENTON*) I think you can supply the missing pieces.

The telephone rings.

FENTON: (*A shade annoyed by the interruption; he lifts the receiver; on the phone*) Yes? … Yes, all right, in about ten minutes.

FENTON replaces the receiver.

CHRISTIE: We can't talk here. Let's meet tonight sometime and have a drink.

FENTON: (*After a moment*) What did you mean just now when you said that – you know certain things which even Scotland Yard don't know?

CHRISTIE: (*Crossing to FENTON; confidentially*) When they found Edward Schroder, there was a packet of cigarettes – 'Mercury' cigarettes – by the side of the body. Am I right?

FENTON: (*Hesitating*) Yes …

CHRISTIE: They also found a packet of cigarettes – 'Mercury' cigarettes – by the body of Mrs Beatrice Terry.

FENTON: Well?

CHRISTIE: Do you know where those cigarettes came from, Mr Fenton? Do you know the significance of the 'Mercury' cigarettes?

FENTON: No …

CHRISTIE: (*Tensely*) Well, I do! You found the first packet of cigarettes in your pocket after you'd operated on Sir Oliver Peters.

FENTON: (*Surprised*) How do you know I operated on Peters?

CHRISTIE: You did, didn't you?

FENTON: (*A moment*) Yes.

118

CHRISTIE: I'll strike a bargain with you. I'll tell you about the cigarettes – I'll tell you all I know, if you'll tell me what really happened the night you operated on Peters.

FENTON hesitates, then suddenly reaches a decision.

FENTON: Yes, all right.

CHRISTIE: Do you know Arlen Court – it's a block of flats in Milton Street, just off the Marylebone Road.

FENTON: I can find it.

CHRISTIE: I'm in Number 24. I'll see you tonight. Six o'clock.

FENTON crosses to the desk.

FENTON: I'll be there.

CHRISTIE: (*Picking up his hat*) Number 24 … Goodbye.

FENTON picks up a pencil and makes a note of the address.

FENTON: Arlen Court, Milton Street …

CHRISTIE: Yes, it's not far from Madame Tussaud's.

FENTON: I'll be there about six.

CHRISTIE: Fine …

CHRISTIE nods and goes out.

FENTON sits at the desk; rises; moves away from the desk, then suddenly turns and opens one of the drawers.

He takes out a London Telephone Directory (E-K) and flicks the pages; after a moment he finds the number he is looking for and, after a slight hesitation, picks up the telephone.

FENTON: (*On the phone*) Get me Central 8005 …

CUT TO: A Newspaper Office

COLLINS, a middle-aged newspaper man, is sitting at an office desk, smoking a pipe; he is quite well dressed, speaks English, and doesn't wear a hat.

The telephone rings and he picks up the receiver.

COLLINS: (*Into the phone*) Collins here … Evening Post … Yes … A Mr Who? … Fenton? … All right,

119

put him on! (*A moment*) Yes, speaking … What can I do for you, Mr Fenton? … Christie? … There's no one here called Christie … Yes, I'm quite sure …I see … Well, he's not on our staff, Mr Fenton … Sorry I can't help you …

COLLINS replaces the receiver.

CUT TO: FENTON's Office. As before.
FENTON replaces the receiver. He looks thoughtful.

CUT TO: Milton Street. Evening; about six o'clock.
A taxi drives up to a modern block of flats.
FENTON gets out of the taxi and after paying the driver he walks to the main entrance of the flats.
On the opposite corner a police car is parked.
DETECTIVE-INSPECTOR AUSTIN and DETECTIVE-INSPECTOR LESTER are in the car together with a plain clothes SERGEANT and a uniformed driver.
They are watching FENTON.

CUT TO: Inside Arlen Court. The front door of
           MICHAEL CHRISTIE's flat.
FENTON rings the door bell of the flat.
A card in a holder is attached to the front door.
The card says: "Mrs and Mrs Michael Christie".
FENTON looks about him; hesitates and is about to ring the bell again when the door is opened by MRS CHRISTIE.
She is very attractive, in a faintly flashy sort of way, and wears a strapless evening gown.
MRS CHRISTIE: (*Pleasantly*) Mr Fenton?
FENTON: Yes.
MRS CHRISTIE: Oh, do come in. I'm awfully sorry to have kept you waiting. My husband is expecting you.

120

FENTON enters the flat.

CUT TO: The Lounge of MICHAEL CHRISTIE's flat.
The room is slightly ornate and over-furnished. There is a cocktail cabinet, tables etc.
There is a cigarette box, lighter and a large photograph of MRS CHRISTIE in a silver frame on the table.
There is a door leading into the bedroom.

MRS CHRISTIE: I'm afraid my husband's out at the moment, Mr Fenton – but (*She looks at her watch*) he promised faithfully to be back by quarter past.

FENTON: I think perhaps I'm a little early.

MRS CHRISTIE: It's just gone six. (*She smiles at FENTON*) Shall I take your hat and coat?

FENTON: (*Hesitating*) Er – thank you.

FENTON takes off his hat and coat and MRS CHRISTIE takes them and puts them down on a chair in the corner of the room.

MRS CHRISTIE: I'm sure Michael won't be long.

MRS CHRISTIE picks up the cigarette box off the table.

MRS CHRISTIE: Would you like a cigarette?

FENTON: Oh, er – thank you.

FENTON takes a cigarette and puts his hand in his pocket for his lighter but MRS CHRISTIE has already flicked the table lighter.

FENTON: Oh, thank you.

A moment.

MRS CHRISTIE looks at FENTON and smiles.

MRS CHRISTIE: Michael tells me you're a surgeon, Mr Fenton.

FENTON: Yes.

MRS CHRISTIE: That must be fascinating work.

FENTON: I think so.

121

MRS CHRISTIE: I have a tremendous admiration for surgeons, and doctors, and nurses, and those sort of people. I just don't know how you do it.

FENTON: Do what, Mrs Christie?

MRS CHRISTIE: Well – cut people up, and look after them, and that sort of thing.

FENTON: You get used to it.

MRS CHRISTIE: Yes, I'm sure you do, but I still think it's wonderful – really wonderful.

FENTON: What do you do, Mrs Christie?

MRS CHRISTIE: Me? (*With a little laugh*) What makes you think I do anything?

FENTON: I'm quite sure you do.

MRS CHRISTIE: If you must know, I'm a singer.

FENTON: (*Dead-pan*) Opera or boogie-woogie?

MRS CHRISTIE looks at FENTON then turns towards the cocktail cabinet.

MRS CHRISTIE: I'm rather versatile.

FENTON turns and watches MRS CHRISTIE.

MRS CHRISTIE: I was just going to have a drink when you arrived, Mr Fenton. What would you like?

FENTON: Well …

MRS CHRISTIE: Martini? Bronx?

FENTON: May I have a Martini?

MRS CHRISTIE: Yes, of course. Dry?

FENTON: Please …

MRS CHRISTIE turns towards the bottle on the cocktail cabinet and takes a bottle of Martini.

FENTON takes stock of his surroundings; his eyes eventually come to rest on the photograph of MRS CHRISTIE on the mantelpiece nearby.

He looks puzzled; picks it up, and stares at the photograph.

MRS CHRISTIE turns and brings FENTON the glass of Martini.

She notices that he is holding the photograph.

MRS CHRISTIE: That was taken by a little man round the corner. I think he's awfully good.

FENTON: (*Looking up*) Yes, it's … a very good photograph of you, Mrs Christie.

MRS CHRISTIE: Michael adores it – he thinks it's quite the best I've ever had.

FENTON: Actually, it was the inscription I was looking at.

MRS CHRISTIE: The inscription?

MRS CHRISTIE stands very close to FENTON and looks at the photograph.

MRS CHRISTIE: "To Michael with love" …?

FENTON: (*Looking at the photograph*) From Gida …

FENTON looks up at MRS CHRISTIE.

She smiles at him.

MRS CHRISTIE: But all my friends call me Gida, Mr Fenton …

END OF EPISODE FOUR

EPISODE FIVE

A CHANGE OF PLAN

OPEN TO: The Lounge of MICHAEL CHRISTIE's Flat.

FENTON and MRS CHRISTIE are looking at the photograph of MRS CHRISTIE which FENTON is holding.

FENTON: Yes, it's … a very good photograph of you, Mrs Christie.

MRS CHRISTIE: Michael adores it – he thinks it's quite the best I've ever had.

FENTON: Actually, it was the inscription I was looking at.

MRS CHRISTIE: The inscription?

MRS CHRISTIE stands very close to FENTON and looks at the photograph.

MRS CHRISTIE: "To Michael with love" …?

FENTON: (*Looking at the photograph*) From Gida …

FENTON looks up at MRS CHRISTIE.
She smiles at him.

MRS CHRISTIE: But all my friends call me Gida, Mr Fenton …

MICHAEL CHRISTIE is standing in the open doorway of the bedroom; he is holding a revolver which is pointing at FENTON.

FENTON turns and looks at MRS CHRISTIE and then at CHRISTIE.

FENTON: (*Quite calmly*) Yes, I've heard the name before.

CHRISTIE: (*With authority*) When? When did you hear the name before?

FENTON: (*Pointing at the revolver*) Is that necessary? I find it rather disconcerting.

CHRISTIE: You'll find it more than disconcerting if you don't answer my question. How did you come to hear the name Gida?

127

FENTON:	I heard it from a man called Wade. He was under the impression that a friend of mine was a friend of yours – or rather of your wife's.
CHRISTIE:	Wade? (*To MRS CHRISTIE*) Who's Wade?
MRS CHRISTIE:	He's the Irishman.
CHRISTIE:	Oh, yes. Did Wade take you to Sir Oliver Peters?
FENTON:	He did.
CHRISTIE:	When?
FENTON:	On two occasions.
MRS CHRISTIE:	Where is Peters?
FENTON:	He's in a house – somewhere in the Cotswolds.
CHRISTIE:	(*Angrily*) What do you mean – somewhere in the Cotswolds? Where is the house?
FENTON:	I don't know.
CHRISTIE:	(*Unable to control himself*) Mr Fenton, I'm not a patient man – even at the best of times. Where is Sir Oliver Peters?
FENTON:	(*Quietly; watching CHRISTIE*) I've told you, I don't know.
CHRISTIE:	(*Obviously determined to fire*) All right.

CHRISTIE raises the revolver.

MRS CHRISTIE:	Wait a minute! (*To FENTON; quietly*) Mr Fenton, please don't underrate us. You operated on Peters so obviously you must know where he is. Now if you've got any sense …
FENTON:	(*Interrupting MRS CHRISTIE*) I haven't the slightest idea where Sir Oliver Peters is. It's perfectly true that I operated on

128

	him; but I was taken to the house in a car and I was blindfolded.
CHRISTIE:	(*Disbelieving FENTON*) On both occasions?
FENTON:	Yes, on both occasions.
CHRISTIE:	Then how do you know the house is in the Cotswolds?
FENTON:	I don't know – not for certain.
CHRISTIE:	(*Watching FENTON*) What makes you think it is?
FENTON:	Well, Sir Oliver said something which rather gave me that impression.
CHRISTIE:	What did he say?
FENTON:	He said … The Golden Valley.
CHRISTIE:	The Golden Valley?
FENTON:	Yes, that's a village – a district – not far from Cirencester.
MRS CHRISTIE:	(*To her husband*) Peters had a house near Cirencester.
CHRISTIE:	Yes, I know. (*He looks at FENTON*) I don't believe you, Fenton. I think you're playing in with Wade. It's my opinion that Peters is here – in London – right under our very noses!
FENTON:	(*A shrug*) You might be right.

Suddenly FENTON throws the contents of his glass at MICHAEL CHRISTIE.

CHRISTIE is taken by surprise.

FENTON then knocks the gun out of his hand; MRS CHRISTIE grabs hold of FENTON as her husband dashes across the room in an attempt to regain possession of the gun.

FENTON has now grabbed hold of MRS CHRISTIE and is using her as a shield.

CHRISTIE moves round the room trying to manoeuvre FENTON into an open position.

FENTON watches him, still holding MRS CHRISTIE.

Suddenly a noise is heard in the hall: the police are forcing the front door.

CHRISTIE looks startled.

AUSTIN's voice: (*Off*) All right, Sergeant.

MRS CHRISTIE: Michael – the police!

CHRISTIE: Stay where you are.

AUSTIN and LESTER rush into the room followed by the plain clothes SERGEANT.

CHRISTIE realises it is the police and immediately rushes into the bedroom and locks the door.

LESTER and the SERGEANT take hold of MRS CHRISTIE.

AUSTIN and FENTON cross to the bedroom door.

AUSTIN tries the handle and hammers on the door.

AUSTIN: Get the door open! (*To MRS CHRISTIE*) Is there a window in there?

As AUSTIN speaks, there is the sound of a revolver shot from inside the bedroom.

There is a pause.

MRS CHRISTIE releases herself and with a sudden cry rushes to the bedroom door.

MRS CHRISTIE: (*Desperately; in tears*) Michael! Michael, open the door! Michael, it's me! It's Gida! Open the door!

LESTER puts his arm on MRS CHRISTIE's shoulder and gently pulls her to one side.

The SERGEANT crosses and throws his weight against the bedroom door.

He breaks the lock and the door is thrown open.

MICHAEL CHRISTIE is lying on the floor, dead – the revolver by his side.

CUT TO: Inside WYMAN's House.

COLONEL WYMAN is sitting at his desk writing a letter; he is smoking a cigar.

He looks thoughtful.

The telephone rings and he lifts the receiver.

WYMAN: (*On the phone*) Hello? … Yes, speaking … Oh, it's you, Inspector … Yes … Yes, of course I will … Where is she? … In your office? … All right, I'll be along in about five minutes … No, of course not. (*He smiles*) If you can't get anything out of her I think it's a very good idea … Well, I'll try, Inspector … All right.

WYMAN replaces the receiver.

He changes his glasses; opens a drawer and takes out a packet of 'Mercury' cigarettes.

He looks at the packet, then puts it in his pocket.

CUT TO: INSPECTOR AUSTIN's Office at Scotland Yard.

AUSTIN stubs his cigarette out in an ashtray on his desk.

MRS CHRISTIE is sitting in a chair facing AUSTIN's desk.

AUSTIN: So you still persist in this story, Mrs Christie?

MRS CHRISTIE: (*Angrily*) I've told you. Mr Fenton came to the flat, he had an appointment to see my husband. When he arrived, Michael – my husband – was out. I asked Mr Fenton in for a drink and he   he …

AUSTIN: Well, go on.

MRS CHRISTIE: I've told you what happened! Surely I don't have to keep on telling you!

AUSTIN: (*Unperturbed*) Go on, Mrs Christie …

MRS CHRISTIE: I – asked Mr Fenton in for a drink and he – tried to kiss me. He was still trying to when Michael arrived.

AUSTIN: And then what happened?

MRS CHRISTIE: I've told you what happened! Michael lost his temper, he thought I was having an affair with Fenton and … he produced a revolver …

AUSTIN: I see. (*Politely*) So that's why your husband threatened to shoot him, because he thought you were having an affair with Mr Fenton?

MRS CHRISTIE: (*Tensely*) Yes.

AUSTIN: You'd seen Mr Fenton before, I take it?

MRS CHRISTIE: Yes, of course. He used to come to the flat pretty regularly.

AUSTIN: Was that the first time he'd tried to kiss you?

MRS CHRISTIE: No – he tried once before.

AUSTIN: (*With authority*) Mrs Christie, your husband saw Mr Fenton for the first time this afternoon – he told him that he was a reporter on The Evening Post and that he was investigating the murder of a man called Edward Schroder: who he thought was mixed up with the disappearance of Sir Oliver Peters. After your husband left the hospital Mr Fenton telephoned the newspaper – I don't have to tell you the rest of the story. As soon as Fenton discovered that he'd been talking to an imposter he got in touch with Scotland Yard. That, of course, is why we were watching the flat.

MRS CHRISTIE: (*Rising*) That's absolute nonsense from start to finish! However, since you obviously choose to believe anything that Mr Fenton tells you …

AUSTIN puts his hand on MRS CHRISTIE's shoulder.

AUSTIN: (*Quietly*) Sit down, Mrs Christie. I've sent for a colleague of mine – a Colonel Wyman. I think he'd like to have a talk to you about – a packet of cigarettes.

MRS CHRISTIE: What do you mean?

AUSTIN: I think you know what I mean – 'Mercury' cigarettes.

A pause.

MRS CHRISTIE: (*Tensely*) Who is this Colonel Wyman?

AUSTIN: I've told you – he's a colleague of mine.

MRS CHRISTIE: Yes, but what does he look like? Is he a middle-aged man with grey hair and rather bad eyesight?

AUSTIN: (*A shade surprised*) Yes …

We now see that COLONEL WYMAN is standing in the doorway.

WYMAN: Distinguished is the word, Mrs Christie.

WYMAN carries a folder containing papers and photographs.

He closes the door.

WYMAN: (*To AUSTIN*) Well?

AUSTIN: (*Shaking his head*) We seem to be on a roundabout.

WYMAN: How very unpleasant.

AUSTIN: She persists in saying that Mr Fenton was having an affair with her. It's a ridiculous story!

WYMAN: Not ridiculous, Inspector.

WYMAN looks admiringly at MRS CHRISTIE.

WYMAN: Untrue, certainly – but not ridiculous.

WYMAN sits on the edge of the desk and looks down at MRS CHRISTIE.

WYMAN: Do you remember me?

MRS CHRISTIE: (*Curtly*) No …

WYMAN: I think you do, Mrs Christie – or should I say Gida? We met in Madrid in 1945. You were in partnership with a man called Barok, a nasty piece of work and highly melodramatic, who ran a criminal organisation known as the 'Mercury' gang.

AUSTIN: (*To WYMAN*) The Mercury gang?

WYMAN: Yes. Barok always introduced himself by producing a packet of cigarettes with the name 'Mercury' on it.

WYMAN takes the packet of cigarettes out of his pocket.

WYMAN: A packet rather like this, Mrs Christie. Barok was arrested, but the nucleus of the 'Mercury' organisation still existed and you came to England and organised an attempt to kidnap Sir Oliver Peters – unfortunately, or fortunately, whichever way you look at it – someone else had the same idea. Peters was kidnapped twenty-four hours before you were able to put your plan into operation. (*He leans forward, towards MRS CHRISTIE*) So you see, Mrs Christie – we've both got the same objective.

MRS CHRISTIE rises; she looks angry and indignant.

MRS CHRISTIE: I don't know what you're talking about! I don't know anything about Peters, except what I've read in the newspapers.

	I've told you the truth; Fenton tried to get fresh with me and Michael resented it. Now, if you don't mind I'd like to go. I've been asked just about enough questions for one day!
AUSTIN:	(*With a sigh; weary*) All right, Mrs Christie, if that's your story.
MRS CHRISTIE:	May I go now?
AUSTIN:	Yes.
MRS CHRISTIE:	And my passport?

AUSTIN picks up a passport off the desk and puts it into a drawer.

AUSTIN:	I'm sorry, I'm afraid I've got to take care of that – for the time being at any rate.

MRS CHRISTIE looks at AUSTIN and hesitates.

WYMAN crosses to the door.

MRS CHRISTIE:	Very well. I shall probably have a word with the Commissioner about it.
AUSTIN:	That's entirely up to you, Mrs Christie.

MRS CHRISTIE crosses to the door, which WYMAN opens for her – and with a look at WYMAN she goes out.

WYMAN closes the door and returns to AUSTIN at the desk.

AUSTIN:	Is that true – about Madrid and the 'Mercury' organisation?
WYMAN:	Yes, course.
AUSTIN:	It's a pity you didn't tell us before.

AUSTIN lifts the telephone receiver and dials.

AUSTIN:	(*On the phone*) She's just leaving … Tell Benson … Right!

AUSTIN replaces the receiver.

WYMAN:	(*Facing AUSTIN; seriously*) Inspector, I had a message from the Home Secretary – just after you telephoned.
AUSTIN:	Well?

135

WYMAN: They've heard – about Peters.

AUSTIN rises and comes round the desk.

WYMAN: Wade's prepared to release him …

AUSTIN: What!

WYMAN: … On one condition. He wants a hundred thousand pounds.

AUSTIN: Good Lord! Is that all?

WYMAN: He points out, not without justification, that we're not the only Government interested in Sir Oliver Peters.

AUSTIN: (*Quietly; a note of urgency in his voice*) Have you told the Commissioner this?

WYMAN: Yes, he knows – he was at the Home Office when they telephoned me.

AUSTIN: (*Exasperated*) Well, what are we going to do? What can we do?

WYMAN: We've got to find Peters and the first thing we've got to do is find that hide-out.

AUSTIN: Yes, but how?

WYMAN: (*Thoughtfully*) I'm afraid we'll have to wait until they get in touch with Fenton again, I don't see any other way. But the moment they do we must be ready. There must be no hold-ups, Inspector! No red-tape!

AUSTIN: (*Briskly; in complete agreement*) For once we see eye to eye.

AUSTIN picks up the telephone receiver.

AUSTIN: I'll brief my department and warn the security people …

WYMAN: (*Quietly*) 'Operation Diplomat' …

AUSTIN nods.

CUT TO: A Corridor is St Mathew's Hospital.

MARK FENTON is walking down the corridor. He enters his office.

CUT TO: FENTON's Office.

FENTON enters the office.

ROBIN TERRY is sitting in an armchair.

He rises as FENTON enters.

FENTON: (*Surprised*) Hello, Mr Terry! They didn't tell me you were here … Hello, what's the matter with your leg?

ROBIN: Oh nothing. I just ricked my ankle last night.

FENTON: I'm sorry. Would you like me to have a look at it?

ROBIN: No thanks, it's all right.

FENTON: Sure?

ROBIN: Yes, really.

FENTON: How long have you been waiting?

ROBIN: Not long.

FENTON looks at his watch.

FENTON: I've been gossiping with the Matron. If I'd known I'd have come straight down. (*He looks at TERRY*) Well – how are you keeping?

ROBIN: Very much better, thank you, but I get some pretty bad headaches.

FENTON: Headaches?

ROBIN: Funnily enough, I only get them at night.

FENTON: Would you like Dr Gillespie to have a look at you?

ROBIN: No. I – don't think so. I expect they'll go. Those sleeping tablets wouldn't cause them, I suppose?

FENTON: (*Shaking his head*) No. How many have you taken?

ROBIN: I took two last night, that's all.

FENTON: (*Nodding*) That's all right. I'll give you something for the headaches.

ROBIN: Mr Fenton, I hate to bother you with my personal affairs, but – I'm rather worried about Linda.

FENTON: Oh?

ROBIN: Did you ever hear her say anything about anyone else, about ... another man, I mean?

FENTON: No, but I've only met your fiancée once, Mr Terry. That was the night your mother was leaving the hospital. You introduced us.

ROBIN: Oh, yes! Yes, of course. (*A shade perplexed*) I'm sorry. I thought she was a friend of yours.

FENTON: Whatever gave you that idea?

TERRY: (*His hand on his head; worried and confused*) I don't know, I'm sure. She came to the hospital quite a lot to see Mardie – and – I must have thought you'd – met her then ...

FENTON: (*Shaking his head*) No. You introduced us.

ROBIN: Yes, of course I did. Mr Fenton, do you mind if I ask you a very blunt question?

FENTON: No ...

ROBIN: That night – the night my mother left the hospital – we got very nearly home and then Linda suddenly remembered that she'd left her gloves behind ...

FENTON: Well?

ROBIN: I don't think she did – I think that was an excuse.

FENTON: An excuse?

ROBIN: Yes ...

FENTON: (*Smiling*) Forgive me – but I don't quite follow.

ROBIN: Did Linda see you again that night? Is that why she returned to the hospital?

FENTON: Look, let's get this straight. Are you accusing me of being – well – 'friendly' with your fiancée?

ROBIN: (*Turning away; a note of desperation in his voice*) Linda's friendly with somebody. I – don't know who it is; but …

FENTON: Well, it isn't me! You can put that idea right out of your head.

ROBIN: (*Looking at FENTON; hesitating*) I'm sorry. It was damn rude of me to suggest it.

FENTON: Look, if you take my advice, you'll go away for a couple of weeks. This business has been a frightful strain on you – it must have been. You want a change – a complete change, I've already told you that.

ROBIN: (*Tensely*) I can't go away, not at the moment. I've been commissioned to paint two pictures, and besides, I – well … (*Facing FENTON*) If I go away what about Linda?

FENTON: Look, if you think Linda is being unfaithful to you, why don't you ask her, quite frankly, whether there is anybody else?

ROBIN: I've – already done so.

FENTON: Well, what did she say?

ROBIN: She – said there wasn't.

FENTON: (*Smiling; dismissing the matter*) Well, there you are! What are you worrying about?

ROBIN: I don't think she was telling me the truth. You see, one night – about a week ago – I suspected that she had a date with somebody and I followed her … I followed her car as far as Burford and then I had a puncture. I asked her

139

the next day why she'd been to Burford and she said she'd never been near the place. (*Tensely*) She was lying!

FENTON: (*Calming ROBIN*) Yes. But there's probably a perfectly simple explanation. Perhaps your fiancée resented being questioned; even wives object to it sometimes, you know! (*A decision*) Look, your nerves are in a very much worse condition than you realise. I'm definitely going to let Dr Gillespie have a look at you.

SISTER ROGERS enters.

SISTER: These are from Mr Robeson.

She puts some X-ray plates on the desk.

FENTON: Oh, thank you, Sister.

SISTER: He said he'd telephone you about four o'clock.

FENTON: Yes, all right. Is Dr Gillespie free at the moment?

SISTER: Yes, I think so, Mr Fenton. He's in his office.

FENTON: Good. I want him to take a look at Mr Terry.

SISTER: Yes, sir.

FENTON: (*To ROBIN*) Now tell Dr Gillespie about those headaches, Mr Terry.

SISTER: (*To ROBIN*) Will you come this way, Mr Terry?

ROBIN: Thank you.

FENTON: I shall probably be upstairs in Ward 3 if you want to see me about anything, Terry.

ROBIN: Thank you.

ROBIN puts his hand across his eyes for a moment, as if in pain, then follows SISTER ROGERS out of the office.

FENTON watches ROBIN, then turns towards the desk and picks up one of the X-ray plates.

The phone rings.

FENTON picks up the receiver.

FENTON: (*On the phone, his thoughts elsewhere, still looking at the X-ray*) Yes? … Yes … speaking …

FENTON suddenly drops the plate on the desk.

FENTON: (*On the phone*) Andrew! … Andrew, how are you? … What's happened?

CUT TO: The Drawing Room in the Country House.

WADE and SEFTON are standing very close together in the drawing room.

PETERS is in the bed in the near background; he is awake and is looking at WADE.

SEFTON is holding the telephone but WADE, who is holding a revolver, takes the phone away from him almost immediately.

SEFTON: (*On the phone*) Yes, I'm all right, but – Wait a minute! Wade wants you …

WADE takes the phone from him.

WADE: (*On the phone*) Fenton? … This is Wade … Listen, this friend of yours – Dr Sefton – tells me that our distinguished guest doesn't need the stuff we were talking about, he needs some stuff called Choro – Choro … (*To SEFTON*) What is it?

SEFTON: Chorodonsatile … But let me talk to him … He won't understand it otherwise …

WADE: (*He hesitates*) All right. But be careful what you say now – don't mention names …

WADE hands the phone to SEFTON.

SEFTON: (*On the phone*) Mark, listen … you know we agreed that you were going to get Chloromphenical for the patient. Well, don't bother, old man. The penicillin's taken effect –

what we need now is Chorodonsatile … Yes, that's right, Chorodonsatile …

CUT TO: FENTON's Office.

FENTON: (*On the phone; puzzled*) Chorodonsatile? But that's ridiculous, Andrew – it wouldn't have any effect on Peters; you know that as well as I do!

CUT TO: Back to SEFTON on the telephone.

SEFTON: (*On the phone*) Yes, I quite agree, old man … I couldn't agree more … (*He looks at WADE*) But in this case, that's the whole point …

WADE: (*To SEFTON*) Here, let me take that!

WADE takes the phone.

WADE: (*On the phone*) Listen, Fenton – do what Sefton tells you. Get this stuff and take it back to your flat; leave the door unlatched … One of us will pick it up tonight about ten o'clock.

CUT TO: FENTON's Office.

FENTON: (*On the phone*) Yes, all right … about ten o'clock.

FENTON replaces the receiver; he looks thoughtful; puzzled.

He shakes his head; after a moment he lifts the receiver again.

FENTON: (*On the phone*) Dr Gillespie, please. (*A moment*) Gillespie? … Fenton here … I'm sorry to bother you, Gillespie, but I wanted to have a word with you. Would you prescribe Chorodonsatile for a case of post-operative infection? Yes … Yes, definitely … No, Chorodonsatile … Well, that's what I thought,

142

absolutely useless … Yes, of course … no, no, no, it's not one of my cases … Yes … Yes, I agree … Well, thanks, Gillespie … Oh – how is Terry? Have you examined him yet? … Well, ring me back.

FENTON replaces the receiver.
He looks thoughtful; he picks up a cigarette off the desk and lights it.

CUT TO: AUSTIN's Office at Scotland Yard.
AUSTIN is sitting at his desk. WYMAN is sitting in a chair opposite, watching him.

WYMAN: I take it Fenton hasn't arrived yet?

AUSTIN: No.

WYMAN: What time did he say he would be here?

AUSTIN: He said six o'clock.

WYMAN: Do you think he's heard from them?

AUSTIN: It sounded very much like it. I've just been reading this report – the one you propose sending to the Home Office.

WYMAN: Well?

AUSTIN: There are still one or two points I don't understand.

WYMAN: Such as?

AUSTIN: Well, after the operation they brought Fenton back to Town.

WYMAN: Yes.

AUSTIN: It was then that he found the packet of cigarettes in his pocket, with the name 'Mercury' on it.

WYMAN: Yes.

AUSTIN: Well, who planted the cigarettes on Fenton? It couldn't have been Gida and it couldn't have been Michael Christie.

143

WYMAN: Wade planted them …

AUSTIN: But why Wade? He wasn't a member of the 'Mercury' organisation?

WYMAN: Wade knew that the 'Mercury' organisation existed and he had a pretty good idea that we knew all about them.

AUSTIN: You mean he planted the cigarettes on Fenton to give the impression that it was the 'Mercury' gang that had picked him up, and that it was the 'Mercury' gang who had Peters?

WYMAN: Exactly. But the thing I don't understand is why they didn't just get rid of Fenton the moment the operation was over.

AUSTIN: But they tried to …

WYMAN: What do you mean?

AUSTIN: Don't you see what happened? Wade told Schroder to poison Fenton, but in actual fact he just doped him. Later, you remember, Schroder went to see Fenton and told him to get out of the country, knowing, of course, that Fenton's life was in danger. Wade discovered that he'd double-crossed him – well, you know what happened to Schroder.

WYMAN: (*Thoughtfully*) Yes … Yes, that seems to make sense, except for the fact that … that Fenton's still alive.

AUSTIN: Of course he is! Soon after Schroder was murdered Peters took an unexpected turn for the worse. They needed a doctor; the obvious choice was Fenton. He'd operated on Peters and knew the case.

WYMAN: Yes … Fenton's been pretty lucky, you know.

AUSTIN: He's also no fool. That was a damn clever move of his to ask for the five hundred pounds.

144

WYMAN: Why?

AUSTIN: Because in Wade's eyes the moment he asked for money he implicated himself. He was no longer a person to be feared ... Ostensibly, at any rate, he was on their side.

WYMAN: Yes ...

WYMAN takes off his glasses; extracts a silk handkerchief from his breast pocket and polishes the glasses.

WYMAN: Austin, do you think Wade is the man behind all this?

AUSTIN: No, I don't. Judging from what Fenton's told us Wade's a tough customer, but he's not the real brains behind this business.

WYMAN: (*Replacing his glasses*) I'm inclined to agree with you.

There is a knock on the door and a uniformed SERGEANT enters.

SERGEANT: Mr Fenton is here, sir.

AUSTIN: All right, Sergeant, show him in.

SERGEANT: Yes, sir.

A pause whilst the SERGEANT goes out.

The SERGEANT returns followed by FENTON.

SERGEANT: Mr Fenton, sir.

The SERGEANT leaves again.

AUSTIN: Come in, Mr Fenton!

FENTON: (*To AUSTIN*) You told me to report to you the moment I heard anything ...

AUSTIN: Yes, indeed ...

WYMAN: What's happened?

FENTON: Wade telephoned me. They want a drug called Chorodonsatile; someone's picking it up tonight – at ten o'clock.

AUSTIN: Where?

FENTON: At my flat ...

145

AUSTIN: Right!

AUSTIN picks up the telephone receiver on his desk.

FENTON: (*Puzzled*) Inspector …

AUSTIN: (*Hesitating*) Yes?

FENTON: There's something I don't understand.

AUSTIN replaces the receiver.

AUSTIN: What do you mean?

FENTON: Well, when we examined Peters both Dr Sefton and myself agreed that he needed Chloromphenical. This afternoon when I got the telephone call Dr Sefton said he wanted Chorodonsatile.

WYMAN: Well?

FENTON: Well, Chorodonsatile isn't any good, it's out of date, we don't use it anymore – in any case it wouldn't have the slightest effect on Peters.

WYMAN: I don't get the point.

FENTON: Well – Dr Sefton must know that; he knows perfectly well that Chorodonsatile isn't any good.

AUSTIN looks at WYMAN; faintly puzzled.

AUSTIN: Did you speak to Dr Sefton, himself?

FENTON: Yes – it was Sefton that actually asked for the Chorodonsatile. That's the extraordinary thing about it.

WYMAN: Did you make any comment? I mean, did you tell him that in your opinion the case didn't call for Chorodonsatile?

FENTON: Yes, of course I told him.

WYMAN: And what did he say?

FENTON: He said – I quite agree, old man – but in this case that's the whole point.

AUSTIN: In this case, that's the whole point?

FENTON: Yes.

AUSTIN: What did he mean by that?

FENTON: I don't know.

AUSTIN: You're sure he understood you?

FENTON: Yes, quite sure.

WYMAN: I gather Wade was standing by his side while all this was going on?

FENTON: Yes, obviously.

WYMAN: Mr Fenton, forgive me – but are you sure about this Chorodonsatile? Would it be useless?

FENTON: Yes, quite useless – and Sefton obviously realised it, that's the point I don't understand.

AUSTIN: Now wait a minute. Let's work this out. First of all, you agreed with Dr Sefton that Peters needed a drug called Chloromphenical. Wade allowed you to come back to Town to get the drug and told you to stand by for instructions. This afternoon he gave you those instructions – but he told you that instead of Chloromphenical they wanted this other stuff. Is that right?

FENTON: Yes.

AUSTIN: (*To WYMAN*) Well, providing we can still follow the contact and rescue Peters I don't see that it makes any difference to us which drug they pick up. (*To FENTON*) Can you get the stuff they want – the Chorodonsatile, I mean?

FENTON: Yes.

AUSTIN: All right. Take it back to your flat and wait for the contact. You needn't do anything else – leave the rest to us, Mr Fenton.

FENTON: All right, Inspector.

FENTON turns towards the door; he is still puzzled.

AUSTIN lifts the telephone.

AUSTIN: (*On the phone*) Extension 89 …

WYMAN: Oh, Mr Fenton …

147

FENTON: (*Turning*) Yes?

WYMAN: Did Dr Sefton say anything else?

FENTON: No, I don't think so. (*Suddenly*) Oh, yes – he said he thought Peters was a little better. I think the penicillin must have helped him.

WYMAN: Good.

AUSTIN: (*On the phone; with authority*) Lester? This is Austin … Listen, I've got Fenton here … It's tonight … Ten o 'clock!

CUT TO: The Drawing Room of FENTON's Flat. Night.

The curtains are drawn and the lights are on.

There is a small package on the table.

LINDA enters through the alcove; she is wearing her outdoor clothes.

She looks round the room.

FENTON comes out of the bedroom.

FENTON: Is this what you're looking for?

LINDA: (*Curtly*) Yes.

LINDA picks up the package and turns towards the alcove.

FENTON: Wait a minute!

LINDA hesitates.

FENTON: How is Peters?

LINDA: (*Unfriendly*) He's a little better – the penicillin seems to have helped him.

FENTON: Did Dr Sefton send any message?

LINDA: No.

FENTON: When are you going to release him?

LINDA: Dr Sefton?

FENTON: Yes.

LINDA: (*Curtly*) I don't know; it's nothing to do with me. I was simply asked to pick this up and take it back to the house.

FENTON: Miss Brooks, there's something I don't quite understand about all this.

LINDA: Is there?

FENTON: Why is Wade taking such a risk? He's never taken one before.

LINDA: What do you mean?

FENTON: You've got the Chorodonsatile, you're taking it back to the house, but – how do you know that I haven't tipped the police off? How do you know that you're not going to be followed?

LINDA: Have you tipped the police off?

FENTON: (*Shaking his head*) No …

LINDA: (*With almost contempt*) Of course you haven't! You're in this business now just as much as Wade or anyone else. I can think of five hundred reasons why you wouldn't go to the police.

FENTON: (*Looking at LINDA; steadily*) Can you, Miss Brooks? Do I detect a note of contempt in your voice, or is it my imagination?

LINDA: (*Facing FENTON; frankly*) Why did you accept the five hundred pounds?

FENTON: I should have thought the reason was obvious. I needed the money.

LINDA: I see.

FENTON: Sit down. I want to talk to you. Please.

They sit on a settee near the fireplace.

FENTON: Have you been to Burford lately?

LINDA hesitates then turns.

LINDA: Burford?

FENTON: Yes.

LINDA: What are you talking about?

FENTON: It's a perfectly simple question; have you been to Burford lately?

149

LINDA: (*Puzzled*) Why, no. I don't think I've ever been there.
FENTON: Oh, now, surely …
LINDA: (*Quite innocently*) Why should I go to Burford?
FENTON: Well, your fiancé seems to think you've got a boyfriend there. I did my best to disillusion him.
LINDA: When … did you see Robin?
FENTON: This afternoon – he came to the hospital. He's not very well, Miss Brooks. It's not surprising.
LINDA: What's the matter with him?
FENTON: For one thing, he's worried about you. He seems to find you somewhat elusive!
LINDA: Yes, I – suppose I have been pretty mean to him. You see, I was engaged to someone else originally and we … broke … it off.
FENTON: Oh? I see.

LINDA looks up at FENTON. She is a shade distressed.

LINDA: I wonder if you do so. (*A moment*) I was engaged to Edward Schroder …
FENTON: (*Surprised*) Schroder!

LINDA nods.

FENTON: Why did you break off the engagement? Was it because he was struck off the register?
LINDA: No, I stood by him through all that business; I'd have continued to stand by him, only …
FENTON: Only what?
LINDA: He met Wade and got mixed up in this Peters affair. He thought – we both thought – it was an easy way of making money. But somehow we just drifted apart and I became engaged to Robin Terry.
FENTON: Why did they kill Schroder?

150

LINDA: Because … he double-crossed them; he had
            instructions to poison you after you'd
            performed the operation on Peters …

LINDA shakes her head; she is near to tears.

LINDA: He couldn't do it, he just couldn't.

FENTON: Why didn't you go to the police when Schroder
            was murdered?

LINDA: I don't know. (*Distressed*) I should have done,
            but – I was so angry, and frightened, I just
            didn't know what to do.

FENTON takes a firm grip of LINDA's arm.

FENTON: Well, you're going to the police now. You're
            going to tell them where Peters is.

LINDA releases her arm; she is frightened.

She rises and walks away from FENTON.

LINDA: No! No, I mustn't! Don't you see, if I do that
            they'll kill me!

FENTON gets up and takes hold of LINDA again.

FENTON: (*Almost angry*) Now listen, Linda … I've no
            illusions about your friend Wade or anyone else
            who's mixed up in this business. The police are
            outside … the whole place is surrounded.
            Whatever happens they'll follow you, so you
            might just as well go to them now.

LINDA: No! No, they mustn't follow me, not tonight!

FENTON: (*Puzzled*) Why?

LINDA: (*Softly*) That's why Wade telephoned you,
            that's why they sent me here … They're testing
            you … They're finding out whether you did go
            to the police or not …

FENTON: What do you mean?

LINDA: I'm to take this packet to a house on the
            outskirts of Stroud … Peters isn't there … He's

nowhere near Stroud … He's not even in the Cotswolds.

FENTON: I see. (*Tensely*) Now I understand why Andrew asked for that stuff instead of Chloromphenical. It was his way of warning me … He was trying to tell me that tonight didn't count … that tonight was only …

FENTON turns and grabs hold of LINDA's arms.

FENTON: (*Tensely*) Linda, listen! This is your chance! You've got to break away from Wade … you've got to take us to that house!

LINDA: No! I can't!

FENTON: You've got to, it is your only chance to get out of this mess.

FENTON takes a firm hold of LINDA and faces her.

FENTON: You've got to take us to Peters.

A moment.

LINDA: All right …

FENTON pats LINDA's arm.

FENTON: Good! (*Quickly; business-like*) Now how did you get here? Did you come by car?

LINDA: Yes.

FENTON: Alone?

LINDA: Yes.

FENTON: Where is it?

LINDA crosses towards the window.

LINDA: I left it on the corner, near Kelwyn Street.

FENTON: Good …

LINDA pulls back the curtains and peers out.

FENTON: Can you see it?

LINDA: Yes. There's another car, over on the other side. A blue limousine …

FENTON: Yes, that's Austin. It's a police car.

As FENTON speaks there is the sound of a revolver shot and the smashing of glass.

LINDA drops the curtains and staggers back from the window.

FENTON: Linda, what is it? What's happened?

FENTON crosses and takes hold of LINDA's arm.

FENTON: Linda!!!

LINDA turns, looks at FENTON for a brief moment, then falls backwards into his arms.

END OF EPISODE FIVE

EPISODE SIX

THE OTHER MAN

OPEN TO: The Drawing Room of FENTON's Flat. Night.

LINDA turns, looks at FENTON for a brief moment, then falls backwards into his arms.
FENTON picks her up and then carries her across the room and goes into the bedroom.
He comes back into the room a few seconds later and crosses into the bathroom: he emerges with a first-aid kit.
He hesitates, then crosses to the window, draws back the curtains, and looks out.
Part of the window is shattered.
He turns and rushes back into the bedroom.

CUT TO: The Bedroom in FENTON's Flat.
LINDA is lying on a single bed; she is conscious, frightened, but not in great pain.
LINDA: Did you – see – anyone?
FENTON: No …
FENTON kneels down and tears LINDA's dress away from her shoulder.
FENTON: Whoever it was must have climbed on to the other balcony … Did you see anyone?
LINDA: No …
FENTON applies some first-aid to LINDA's wound.
FENTON: Is that hurting?
LINDA: A little. I – I think it's just … my shoulder …
FENTON: We'll have to get you to the hospital. Now don't worry, Linda … You'll be all right.
FENTON looks down at LINDA for a moment, then moves away from the bed.

CUT TO: The Drawing Room in FENTON's Flat.
FENTON enters and crosses to the telephone.
He dials – the number is engaged.

157

He looks towards the bedroom and replaces the receiver.
He then picks it up again and dials 'O' for the operator.

FENTON: (*On the phone*) Hello? Miss … I want Sloane
                    300, but it's engaged. It's extremely urgent –
                    there's been an accident here. Would you ring
                    me back when the number's free? … Thank
                    you.

FENTON replaces the receiver and returns to the bedroom.

CUT TO: The Bedroom in FENTON's Flat.

FENTON enters and kneels by the bed.

FENTON: Don't worry, as soon as we get you to hospital
                    you'll be all right.

LINDA looks up at FENTON; she is near to tears.

LINDA: I don't know who it was that fired that shot, but
                    …

FENTON: Don't talk, Linda. Just try and keep still.

LINDA: (*Wincing; she is now obviously in pain*) Mr
                    Fenton, I've got to tell you this, just in case …
                    something happens to me … That house, the
                    house where they've got Peters …

FENTON: Yes?

LINDA: It's … not in the Cotswolds, it's … a house
                    called Blackfield, it's … just off … Kingston
                    Hill.

FENTON: (*Surprised*) Kingston Hill?

LINDA: Yes … we used to drive round for two or three
                    hours so … that …

LINDA closes her eyes; she is obviously in pain.

LINDA: … you'd think the house was miles out of
                    Town.

The telephone can be heard ringing in the drawing room.

158

CUT TO: The Drawing Room in FENTON's Flat.

FENTON enters and answers the telephone.

FENTON: (*On the phone*) Hello? … Oh, thank you …
           Hello? … This is Mr Fenton – put me through
           to Extension 34 … Hello? Is that you Bennett?
           This is Mr Fenton … Listen, I want an
           ambulance at my flat – straight away …
           You've got the address? … No, no, I'm all
           right … Yes, it's urgent!

FENTON replaces the receiver.

*He turns towards the bedroom and as he does so, the front
door bell rings.*

He goes to the door and opens it.

ROBIN TERRY enters.

The door is left open.

ROBIN: Where's Linda?

FENTON: (*After a moment, quietly, nodding towards the
           bedroom*) She's in there.

*ROBIN looks at FENTON for a moment then goes into the
bedroom.*

FENTON stands quite still, watching the door.

ROBIN's voice: (*From the bedroom*) Linda, darling!
           What is it? What's happened?

There is a slight pause.

ROBIN comes out of the bedroom; he looks frightened.

ROBIN: What's happened, Fenton? What have you
           done?

FENTON: Terry, listen! I can't explain now but your
           fiancée came here tonight because …

ROBIN: I know why she came here, Fenton – you don't
           have to tell me! I knew it was you she wanted
           to see that night when she went back to the
           hospital.

FENTON takes hold of ROBIN's arm.

159

FENTON: Terry, listen! Don't be a fool! I tell you there's nothing between us, absolutely nothing!

ROBIN: Then why did she come here?

FENTON: Terry, for heaven's sake, listen!

A slight pause.

FENTON: Linda's been shot.

ROBIN: (*Staggered*) Shot!

FENTON: Yes. She was standing in front of the window; there was somebody on the balcony and …

ROBIN: Who was on the balcony? Who shot her?

FENTON: I don't know …

ROBIN: (*Tensely*) I don't believe you, Fenton! I don't believe this story!

FENTON: Good Lord, man, why should I lie to you?

ROBIN looks at FENTON for a moment and then crosses over to the window.

He opens the window and goes out onto the balcony.

He picks up a pair of spectacles.

FENTON: What is it? What have you got there?

ROBIN: It's a pair of spectacles. Someone must have dropped them … They were on the balcony.

FENTON: Let me see them.

FENTON takes the spectacles and examines them; he is obviously surprised.

FENTON: (*A note of urgency in his voice*) Terry, listen! I want you to go downstairs. You'll see a blue car parked on the corner of the street …

ROBIN: I'm not leaving you here with Linda.

FENTON: Don't be a fool and listen. Go downstairs –

FENTON stops speaking.

There is the sound of voices in the hall.

DETECTIVE-INSPECTOR AUSTIN enters with COLONEL WYMAN.

WYMAN is wearing his glasses.

AUSTIN: (*Quickly; to FENTON*) Fenton, what the devil's happened? What's holding you up? (*Surprised; he notices TERRY*) Oh, hello, Terry! (*He looks at FENTON again; curious*) What's happened?

FENTON: Miss Brooks has been shot!

AUSTIN: Shot!

WYMAN: (*Quickly, to AUSTIN*) I thought I heard a shot! It was just after I left the car …

AUSTIN: (*To FENTON; quickly*) Where is she?

FENTON: In the bedroom. I shouldn't disturb her, Inspector. I've sent for an ambulance.

AUSTIN: Is it serious?

FENTON: (*Looking at TERRY*) No … I don't think so …

AUSTIN looks at WYMAN and decides to ignore FENTON's advice. He goes into the bedroom.

WYMAN: (*To FENTON*) Well – what happened?

FENTON: Much the same sort of thing that happened to Schroder. She crossed over to the window and there was someone on the balcony.

WYMAN looks at FENTON for a moment and then crosses to the window.

ROBIN watches him.

WYMAN looks out onto the balcony and then turns back into the room.

WYMAN: (*To FENTON; almost a note of sarcasm in his voice*) Did you see this – person – on the balcony, Mr Fenton?

FENTON: No …

There is the sound of an ambulance bell from the street below.

WYMAN: Did Miss Brooks?

FENTON: No – at least if she did, she didn't recognise him.

WYMAN: I see.

AUSTIN comes out of the bedroom.

AUSTIN: (*To FENTON*) The ambulance has arrived.

FENTON: I'd better go down and tell them where we are.

AUSTIN: (*With quiet authority*) Wait a moment. (*To TERRY*) Would you go down, please, Mr Terry? I want to have a word with Mr Fenton.

ROBIN looks at FENTON then across at the INSPECTOR.

ROBIN: Yes – all right.

ROBIN goes.

FENTON crosses to AUSTIN.

FENTON: (*Urgently*) Inspector, she's told me where Peters is! He's not in the Cotswolds! He's in a house on Kingston Hill.

AUSTIN: (*Interrupting FENTON*) Yes, I know … she's just told me. How long has Terry been here?

FENTON: Oh – just a few moments.

AUSTIN: Did you expect him?

FENTON: No, of course not.

AUSTIN: Then what was he doing here?

FENTON: (*After a slight hesitation*) He – followed Miss Brooks here – he thought I was having an affair with her.

AUSTIN: I see. Who has the flat on the other side of this – the one with the adjoining balcony?

FENTON: It's let to an American called Streather. He's in Washington at the moment.

AUSTIN: (*Looking at WYMAN*) Oh … How long has he been away?

FENTON: About two months, I should say.

AUSTIN: I see.

AUSTIN turns towards the balcony.

FENTON: Colonel Wyman.

WYMAN: Yes?

FENTON: Have you lost your spectacles?

162

WYMAN: You can see I haven't – I'm wearing them.

FENTON: I thought you had another pair?

WYMAN: I have – for reading.

FENTON: (*After a moment; hesitatingly*) Could I see them? The second pair?

WYMAN: (*After a tiny pause*) Certainly.

WYMAN takes the second pair of spectacles out of his breast pocket.

He holds them so that they can be seen quite clearly by FENTON.

WYMAN smiles.

CUT TO: AUSTIN's Office at Scotland Yard.

AUSTIN is standing behind his desk and in front of a large scale map of the Kingston-upon-Thames area. He is addressing a large body of plain clothes men.

AUSTIN: We have just received information about Sir Oliver Peters! We now know exactly where he is. Instructions are being issued to the Flying Squad, all central C.I.D. departments, local stations, and the Special Branch!

AUSTIN looks at his watch.

AUSTIN: These are your final details for – Operation Diplomat!

CUT TO: A Corridor at Scotland Yard

COLONEL WYMAN walks down the corridor and stops at the point where a telephone is mounted on the wall.

He looks down the corridor to see if there is anyone in sight, takes off his glasses, changes them, and turns towards the telephone.

He lifts the receiver and starts to dial.

CUT TO: The Drawing Room in The Country House

SIR OLIVER PETERS is sitting up in bed.

The AMBULANCE NURSE is preparing him for an injection.

DR SEFTON is preparing the actual injection.

The telephone starts to ring.

WADE, with a revolver in his hand, is watching SEFTON.

The NURSE stops her work and looks up anxiously as the telephone rings.

DR SEFTON turns and looks at the telephone and then at WADE.

WADE crosses over and answers the telephone.

WADE: (*On the phone*) Hello? … Yes … (*Worried*) …
           Who is that? … Oh, I didn't recognise your
           voice … (*Quickly*) Look, I'm worried …
           Harrison hasn't returned yet … (*Surprised*)
           What? … Yes … I'm listening … (*Excited*) …
           When did you hear from them? … (*Delighted*)
           Why man, that's grand news! … Grand! …
           Don't worry, he'll be ready all right – I'll see to
           that! … O.K. … Ring me back as soon as you
           know … Right!

WADE replaces the receiver.

He turns towards the bed, looking very pleased with himself.

The NURSE, SIR OLIVER and SEFTON are staring at WADE – obviously curious about the telephone call.

WADE: What are you all staring at?

NURSE: Who was that?

WADE: Who do you think?

NURSE: Was it …?

WADE: (*Quickly*) Yes!

NURSE: (*Nervously*) What's happened? Is everything all
           right?

WADE: (*Pleased with himself*) Yes … Yes, everything's fine. (*To SEFTON*) Make that a good one now … We may be moving him soon …

PETERS: Moving me? Where are you taking me to? What … are you going to do with me?

SEFTON: (*To PETERS; softly*) It's all right, sir. Now, please, don't excite yourself.

NURSE: (*To WADE; tensely*) What's happened? What did he say?

A moment.

SEFTON looks at WADE.

WADE: (*To SEFTON*) Give him the injection.

SEFTON hesitates; turns and completes the preparation of the injection.

He turns towards the bed and bends over SIR OLIVER – about to give the injection.

WADE sits in an armchair watching SEFTON.

SEFTON straightens himself; the NURSE dabs cotton wool on SIR OLIVER's arm.

SEFTON: (*To PETERS*) Did that hurt?

PETERS: No … no, that's all right, doctor.

WADE: (*To SEFTON*) O.K.?

SEFTON: Yes.

WADE rises and moves across and sits on the bed.

WADE: Well, I don't suppose there's any reason why I shouldn't tell you. It looks as if you'll be leaving us soon, Sir Oliver.

PETERS: Where are you taking me?

SEFTON: (*To WADE*) What's happened?

WADE: (*Looking down at PETERS: smiling at him*) We've had an offer for you. Fifty thousand pounds …

CUT TO: The Drawing Room in the Country House.
            Later.

SIR OLIVER PETERS is sitting up in bed; he is awake but still looks very ill.

DR SEFTON and the NURSE are standing by his side.

The NURSE has her arm round PETERS' shoulder; supporting him.

They have been trying to get SIR OLIVER out of bed but it is obvious that he is far too ill.

SEFTON: (*To PETERS*) Are you in pain, sir?

PETERS: Just – just a little … I shall feel better in a
          moment …

SEFTON: It's all right, Sir Oliver – don't worry. Now just
          take it easy. (*To the NURSE*) Get me that
          cushion!

The NURSE crosses and gets a cushion from one of the chairs.

SEFTON takes the cushion from her and puts it behind PETERS – propping him up.

SEFTON: Is that better?

PETERS: Yes.

NURSE: We've got to get him up! Wade said that …

SEFTON: Never mind what Wade said! So far as Sir
          Oliver is concerned – I'm giving the orders.

WADE enters.

He is wearing a dark overcoat.

He is a little surprised to find PETERS still in bed.

WADE: (*To SEFTON*) I thought I told you to get him
          up?

SEFTON: We've tried – it's impossible. He's not fit
          enough.

WADE looks at the NURSE; crosses to the main door, takes a key out of his pocket, and unlocks it.

He returns and takes a revolver out of his coat pocket.

166

WADE: (*To SEFTON*) Get him up …

SEFTON: I've told you, it's impossible. He's far too ill. If he gets up now he'll have a relapse. I won't be responsible.

WADE: No one's asking you to be responsible, Dr Sefton. Now get him up!

SEFTON: I've told you, it's impossible!

PETERS: (*Slowly; tired*) Let me try again, doctor. Perhaps if I get my feet on the ground I shall … feel … stronger …

SEFTON: (*Determined*) No … (*To WADE*) If you want to move Sir Oliver, you'll move him in an ambulance.

WADE: We haven't got an ambulance! Now listen, Dr Sefton – at any moment I'm expecting that telephone to ring. I'm expecting to be told where we've got to take Peters.

SEFTON: He can't be moved – except by ambulance.

WADE: I've told you – we haven't got an ambulance!

SEFTON: Then get one!

There is the sound of a car in the courtyard outside.

NURSE: It's a car!

WADE: It's Linda! Go down and tell her what's happened! Don't let her put the car away.

The NURSE leaves.

WADE: (*To SEFTON*) Supposing we get a stretcher, and put him in the back of a car?

SEFTON: We haven't got a stretcher.

WADE: (*Angrily*) Supposing we get one!?

SEFTON moves round the bed and joins WADE.

SEFTON: I don't like it.

WADE: I didn't ask you whether you liked it or not! Is it a possibility?

SEFTON: Yes, it's a possibility, but of course he might have a relapse.

WADE: We'll have to take that risk.

As WADE speaks there is a sudden scream from the NURSE who has now reached the courtyard and has recognised the police.

WADE looks at SEFTON, then dashes to the window and looks out.

WADE: (*Amazed*) Good God! It's the police!

WADE turns away from the window; bewildered and confused.

SEFTON immediately takes advantage of the situation and throws himself at WADE.

WADE raises the revolver – but SEFTON has already taken a firm grip on WADE's right arm.

They struggle for possession of the revolver.

SEFTON forces WADE across the room and he falls backwards, against the bed.

SEFTON twists WADE's arm as far as it will go and WADE is forced to drop the revolver – onto the bed.

WADE makes a last desperate effort and forces SEFTON away from him.

WADE turns and rushes for the door.

SIR OLIVER PETERS is sitting up in bed and has now picked up the revolver.

He slowly raises it and points it at WADE.

WADE turns and sees SIR OLIVER pointing the revolver at him.

He is terrified.

WADE: No! No! Don't fire! Don't fire! For God's sake, don't fire!!!

A shot is fired.

CUT TO: Various Newspaper Banner Headlines:
"MISSING DIPLOMAT FOUND"
"PETERS IN LONDON"
"OPERATION DIPLOMAT – PETERS FOUND"

CUT TO: The Drawing Room in FENTON's Flat.
The curtains are drawn.
The door bell is ringing.
FENTON comes out of the kitchen and crosses to the alcove.
FENTON opens the front door.
ROBIN TERRY is standing in the doorway; he carries a soft
hat and the evening newspaper; he is leaning on a walking
stick.

FENTON: Hello, Terry!

ROBIN: May I come in?

FENTON: (*Hesitating*) Er – yes, of course.

ROBIN: Have you a date this evening?

FENTON: Yes, I'm due at the hospital at seven o'clock.
           Why?

ROBIN: Oh – I was wondering if we could have dinner
           together, there are one or two things I want to
           talk to you about.

FENTON: What sort of things?

ROBIN: Well – for one, I want to apologise.

FENTON: Apologise? What for?

ROBIN: For all I said about you and Linda.

FENTON: Oh, forget it!

FENTON turns to the drinks table.

FENTON: You were overwrought. I never took you
           seriously anyway.

FENTON indicates the drinks.

FENTON: Would you like a drink?

ROBIN: (*Hesitating*) Well –

FENTON: I can recommend the sherry.

169

ROBIN: Thank you.

FENTON pours TERRY a glass of sherry and then gives it to him; he pours himself a glass.

FENTON: How are you feeling? Do you still get those
  .   headaches?

ROBIN: Yes, but they're not quite so bad.

FENTON: Good.

FENTON nods at TERRY's stick.

FENTON: How's your ankle?

ROBIN: I twisted it yesterday afternoon. It was pretty
             painful at the time, but it's not so bad now.

FENTON: Would you like me to have a look at it?

ROBIN: Oh, it's really all right now. (*Pause*) Fenton,
             why won't they let me see Linda?

FENTON: Haven't you seen her?

ROBIN: No. I've been to the hospital several times, but
             they've refused to let me see her.

FENTON: Oh. Well, perhaps you've called at the wrong
             time. We have special visiting hours at the
             hospital, you know. You can't just drop in
             whenever you feel like it.

ROBIN: I know the visiting hours. Don't forget I used to
             visit my mother. What is the real reason?

FENTON: The real reason?

ROBIN: (*A note of anger in his voice*) Why won't they
             let me see my fiancée?

A moment.

FENTON: She doesn't want to see you.

ROBIN: Did she tell you that?

FENTON: No, she told Dr Sefton.

ROBIN: I don't believe it! Sefton's lying!

FENTON: Don't be silly! Why should he lie? Sefton's not
             personally interested in you or Miss Brooks.

ROBIN: Then why can't I see her?

FENTON: I've told you why – she doesn't want to see
you.

ROBIN: Fenton, I've got to see Linda! I've got to talk to
her! I've got to find out how she … (*Holding
out the newspaper*) … got mixed up in this
Peters affair.

FENTON: We know how she got mixed up in it, Terry.
She was engaged to a man called Edward
Schroder.

ROBIN: Well?

FENTON: Schroder was a qualified doctor and a friend of
Wade's.

ROBIN: Wade? Oh, yes … He was the man who
kidnapped Peters. He kept Peters in a house on
Kingston Hill. I've just been reading about it.

FENTON: Yes.

ROBIN: But, Fenton, it says here that Wade used to live
at the Polygon Club.

FENTON: Yes, I believe he did.

ROBIN: But that's where my mother – was murdered!

FENTON: Well?

ROBIN: Well – was that … just a coincidence, or was
my mother mixed up in this affair?

FENTON faces TERRY, but he doesn't reply.

ROBIN: Well – was she?

FENTON: Yes.

ROBIN: Oh!

FENTON: I think I'd better tell you everything, Terry. I
saw Inspector Austin this afternoon. He told me
what happened the night your mother went to
the Polygon Club.

ROBIN: Well?

FENTON: I'm afraid this is going to be something of a
shock to you, Terry, but you've got to know the

171

facts sooner or later. Your mother was just as much involved in this business as Linda. She knew that I'd been picked up by Wade and made to operate on Peters. She also knew that from the moment I performed the operation my life was in danger.

ROBIN: Go on.

FENTON: Your mother was a curious woman. She was hard and cruel in many ways, but fortunately for me, she had a soft streak. She decided to warn me. She gave me a note telling me to ring a certain number and order two dozen carnations. I rang the number and Wade, who was a friend of your mother's, told me to go to the Polygon Club. Your mother meant to meet me there, of course, that's why she went.

ROBIN: But why didn't she simply talk to you at the hospital?

FENTON: Because she only heard about my operating on Peters the night she left the hospital and there just wasn't an opportunity for her to speak to me. Besides she knew she was being watched and her only chance was to get me alone somewhere and explain the whole situation. The Polygon Club was the perfect rendezvous – who would expect to find your mother or "Mr Fenton" at the Polygon Club?

ROBIN: Yes, I can see that, but didn't she take a risk giving you a note?

FENTON: Of course she didn't. If I'd been murdered – 'accidentally' knocked down by a car for instance – all the police would have found on me was a note from your mother asking me to order some flowers.

ROBIN: What did happen at the Polygon Club? Did you see my mother?

FENTON: No – at least, not until after she was murdered. She was followed to the Polygon Club by a Colonel Wyman. He saw her enter the club and he waited for her to come out. Unfortunately, Wade double-crossed your mother and told someone else about her appointment with me. That someone else was already at the club when your mother arrived.

ROBIN: And was he the man who murdered her?

FENTON: Yes.

ROBIN: Go on.

FENTON: Wyman got tired of waiting and decided to investigate. He found your mother – by the side of the body was a packet of 'Mercury' cigarettes. They had been planted there by the murderer to throw suspicion on to the Christies.

ROBIN: You mean the Gida gang?

FENTON: They were, of course, interested in doing a deal over Peters. Wyman picked up the packet of cigarettes and then decided to search the bedroom. It was while he was in the bedroom that I arrived …

ROBIN: But this man who murdered my mother … Was it Wade?

FENTON: No. I've told you. Wade was a friend of your mother's – at least he was until he double-crossed her and told this other man about her appointment at the Polygon Club.

ROBIN: But who was this other man?

FENTON: (*Watching TERRY; a note of tenseness in his voice*) He was the man who organised the kidnapping of Peters; the man that Wade and

	Linda and your mother and the rest of the small fry took their orders from.
ROBIN:	You still haven't answered my question – who was he?

A moment.

FENTON:	(*Quietly*) Terry, you remember when Linda was shot?
ROBIN:	Yes.
FENTON:	You arrived shortly afterwards.
ROBIN:	Yes.
FENTON:	How did you get into the building?
ROBIN:	Why – I came through the front door, of course.
FENTON:	Did you? No one saw you.
ROBIN:	What do you mean?
FENTON:	The police were outside: they were watching the building.
ROBIN:	What are you suggesting?
FENTON:	I'm suggesting that you were already here – on the balcony! You knew that Linda was coming here to pick up the Chorodonsatile and you intended to check up on her. As soon as you'd fired the shot you climbed into the adjoining balcony and came through the flat next door.
ROBIN:	And what about the spectacles – the ones I found on the balcony?
FENTON:	You planted them there to give the impression that the man on the balcony had been wearing glasses.
ROBIN:	Fenton, are you crazy? Why you must be out of your mind even to suggest such a thing!
FENTON:	(*Slowly; watching TERRY*) Colonel Wyman has a rather curious hobby, Terry. He's a ventriloquist.

ROBIN clutches the handle of his walking stick.

174

ROBIN: Go on.

FENTON: He can also, when the occasion demands it, do a spot of impersonating. He impersonated you.

ROBIN: How very interesting. When?

FENTON: He phoned Wade and said an offer had been made for Sir Oliver Peters. Wade thought it was you. He gave the game away.

ROBIN: A very interesting account, Fenton, but not quite complete. I think I'd better complete it for you. Everything would have worked out according to plan but for one fact – certain people couldn't help interfering. You found one of them here in your flat – Schroder, and another at the Polygon Club. What a pity you've chosen to interfere too.

TERRY steps back and suddenly draws a knife out of the head of the walking stick.

FENTON sees the knife, and instinctively steps back, away from TERRY.

FENTON: Don't be a fool, Terry! Put that knife down!

FENTON moves back as TERRY slowly advances towards him.

Suddenly TERRY raises his arm – he is about to strike.

There is the sound of a revolver shot and TERRY gives a cry of pain, drops the knife, and clutches his wrist.

We then see that WYMAN is standing in the doorway, revolver in hand.

CUT TO: FENTON's Office at St Mathew's Hospital.

SISTER ROGERS is sitting at the desk writing in a notebook.

The door opens and DR SEFTON enters; he wears his hospital clothes.

SISTER ROGERS rises.

SEFTON: It's all right, Sister! Don't get up.

SISTER: Has Sir Oliver gone?

SEFTON: He's just leaving. Mr Fenton's saying goodbye to him.

SISTER: He's an extraordinary character; got a heavenly sense of humour. He had us in fits of laughter last night.

SEFTON: Yes, so I heard.

SISTER: He's made an amazing recovery.

SEFTON: Yes – of course he was lucky. He had a jolly good doctor.

SISTER: (*Amused*) By the way, Dr Gillespie would like you to write a report on the Peters case.

SEFTON: Would he? Well, when I write a report on the Peters case it won't be for Dr Gillespie. (*Laughing*) It'll be for the Sunday newspapers. (*Suddenly*) You know that's quite an idea! I could pep it up a bit – give it a real sexy angle. Turn the nurse into a sort of Mata Hari.

SISTER ROGERS gives SEFTON a look.

SISTER: Yes, well don't you turn me into a sort of Mata Hari, Dr Sefton!

SEFTON: (*Laughing*) Forever Rogers – or the Secrets of a Sinful Sister!

MARK FENTON enters followed by DETECTIVE-INSPECTOR AUSTIN.

FENTON: Ah, yes, here's your things.

SISTER ROGERS rises and picks up AUSTIN's hat and gloves off one of the chairs.

AUSTIN takes them.

AUSTIN: Oh, thank you, Sister.

SISTER ROGERS leaves.

AUSTIN turns towards FENTON.

AUSTIN: Well, I'll say goodbye, Mr Fenton.

FENTON: Inspector, before you go – there are one or two things – about this Peters affair – that I don't quite understand.

AUSTIN: For instance?

FENTON: Well – what gave Sir Oliver the impression that the house was in the Cotswolds – when in actual fact it was on Kingston Hill?

AUSTIN: When they kidnapped Peters they blindfolded him, of course, and then deliberately took about two and a half hours over a journey which would normally take about half an hour.

FENTON: So I was right about that!

AUSTIN: They also firmly planted in his mind – by making quite sure he overheard snatches of conversations - that the house was in the Cotswolds – in Charlesworth, in fact. That he was in the Cotswolds by letting him hear the chimes of a church clock. Sir Oliver immediately recognised the clock as the one at Charlesworth – his local village. What he didn't recognise, however, was the fact that it was a recording. We found that recording when we searched the house.

FENTON: I see.

AUSTIN: (*Amused*) But, quite unwittingly, the old boy very nearly foxed them. Being a local he's always thought of Charlesworth as The Golden Valley. He said – the Golden Valley – to you, Mr Fenton – instead of simply Charlesworth or the Cotswolds.

SEFTON: (*To AUSTIN*) Is that why Terry gave Mark the picture – to make sure that he knew where the Golden Valley was?

177

AUSTIN: (*Laughing*) Yes. He didn't want him to think it was on Kingston Hill! And that's why Terry told you that he'd followed Linda out to Burford – you see, once again, he was pointing towards the Cotswolds.

FENTON: So Sir Oliver really thought he was in Charlesworth?

AUSTIN: Yes; of course once they'd convinced Peters the rest was easy.

SEFTON: I suppose what they really wanted was Sir Oliver to say – "I'm in the Cotswolds" – instead of which the old boy said – "Golden Valley" …

AUSTIN: (*Laughing*) Exactly!

FENTON: Inspector …

AUSTIN: Yes?

FENTON: What's going to happen to Linda Brooks?

AUSTIN: (*Thoughtfully*) She'll get two or three years – if she's lucky.

FENTON: She'll be well enough to leave the hospital on Thursday.

AUSTIN: Yes – so Dr Gillespie told me.

AUSTIN shakes hands with FENTON.

AUSTIN: Well – that's not my problem, thank goodness.

WYMAN enters and stands in the doorway.

WYMAN: (*To AUSTIN*) Peters is ready – we're just leaving.

AUSTIN: Right!

FENTON: (*Smiling*) Are you the bodyguard?

WYMAN: Yes – although we prefer to be known as the reception committee.

WYMAN shakes hands with FENTON and DR SEFTON.

WYMAN: Well, goodbye, Mr Fenton. I hope we shall meet again sometime.

FENTON: I hope so.

WYMAN: (*To SEFTON*) Goodbye, doctor. I'll give you a ring – we'll fix up a game of golf one day.

SEFTON: Splendid!

The telephone rings on FENTON's desk.

AUSTIN: Goodbye, Mr Fenton! (*To SEFTON*) Goodbye, doctor!

AUSTIN and WYMAN leave.

FENTON crosses to the desk and answers the phone.

FENTON: (*On the phone*) Hello? … Yes … Oh, hello, sir! You got my letter? … Yes … Yes, I'm afraid so, sir. (*A moment*) Well, that's very nice of you, Sir John – I appreciate it … Thank you … Yes, I will … Yes, by all means … Thank you for ringing … Goodbye, sir.

FENTON replaces the receiver and crosses to the window.

SEFTON looks at FENTON; faintly puzzled.

SEFTON: Was that the Chairman – His Royal Highness, himself?

FENTON doesn't turn: he is looking out of the window.

FENTON: Yes …

SEFTON: They're just leaving …

CUT TO: Outside St Mathew's Hospital.

SIR OLIVER, WYMAN and AUSTIN are leaving the hospital. They turn, look up at the building, and wave at FENTON at the window.

CUT TO: FENTON's Office. As before.

SISTER ROGERS enters with an X-ray plate.

She crosses to SEFTON.

SISTER: Dr Gillespie asked me to give you this, doctor. He's in Ward 3 if you need him.

SEFTON: (*Still looking at FENTON*) Thank you, Sister.

179

SISTER ROGERS looks at SEFTON, then across at FENTON.

FENTON waves back to the group below, then turns and crosses back to his desk.

He looks at the SISTER and SEFTON.

FENTON: Well?

SEFTON: That's the end of – Operation Diplomat.

FENTON: Yes.

SEFTON: Back to the grindstone! (*Laughing*) And I can't say I'm sorry.

SEFTON looks at the X-ray plate he is holding.

FENTON: (*Quietly*) Andrew …

SEFTON: (*Looking up*) Yes, old boy?

FENTON: Sister Rogers …

SISTER: Yes, Mr Fenton?

FENTON: I've written Sir John Waverley a letter. I'm resigning from the staff.

SISTER: (*Surprised*) Why, Mr Fenton!

SEFTON: (*Astonished*) Why the devil have you done that?

FENTON: Oh, I don't know. I've been here quite a while now, Andrew. I think it's about time I made a change.

SISTER: But what are you going to do, Mr Fenton?

FENTON: (*Smiling*) I've taken rooms in Wimpole Street. I'm going into private practice.

SEFTON: (*Delighted*) Are you, by George? Congratulations, Mark!!

SISTER: (*Pleased*) Good for you, Mr Fenton!

FENTON puts his arm round SEFTON's shoulder and SISTER ROGERS'.

FENTON: It's a gamble, I know – but I've decided to take it. (*Laughing*) Besides, things are getting too exciting round here. Ever since I've been at St

180

Mathew's I've been in a mad whirl of mystery and intrigue! After all, nothing very exciting can happen in private practice – especially in Wimpole Street.

SISTER ROGERS and SEFTON give FENTON a definite look.

SEFTON: (*With a very 'knowing' nod*) That's what you think, old boy!

THE END

Press Pack
Press cuttings about Operation Diplomat ...

Operation Diplomat by **Francis Durbridge**

Before you see the first episode of *Operation Diplomat* there are two points I should like to make quite clear. The first is that though the principal character is Mark Fenton, a surgeon at St Mathew's Hospital, the actual story is not a sequel to *The Broken Horseshoe*. The second point is that although *Operation Diplomat* evolves round the strange disappearance of a missing diplomat the story is not based on any actual incident and was not suggested or even inspired by the mysterious disappearance of Guy Burgess and Donald MacLean.

Operation Diplomat starts when Mark Fenton reads that Sir Oliver Peters, a prominent top-secret diplomat, has mysteriously disappeared and is in turn reported to have been seen in Helsinki, Prague, Bucharest, the Eastern Zone of Berlin, and Moscow! Sir Oliver is a man of about sixty with an intimate knowledge of European affairs and Western defence. He was educated at Eton and is a graduate of Harvard University; for several years he was Ambassador to one of the major European Powers. At the beginning of 1951 he was taken ill, moved to St Mathew's Hospital and operated on by Mark Fenton.

During the period of convalescence Fenton had several conversations with Sir Oliver and a brief, casual friendship sprang up between the surgeon and the diplomat. The word 'Operation' in the title has a double meaning, it refers to 'operation' in both the surgical and the military sense.

Although the story is pure fiction and has no message or political significance this does not mean that it is a far-fetched story completely divorced from reality. On the contrary, I feel quite sure that everything that takes place in the story could – and probably has! – actually happened at some time or other. A great many viewers wrote to me during the run of my first television serial to point out that, by a remarkable coincidence, the police had discovered that a horse doping organisation were actually obtaining their drugs through a secret organisation like the one depicted in *The Broken Horseshoe*.

The part of Mark Fenton will on this occasion be played by Hector Ross who theatregoers will remember in Terence Rattigan's *Playbill* and the Duke of York's success *Larger Than Life*. Viewers, of course, will remember him for his performances in *The Devil's Disciple*, *The Guinea Pig* and *No Birds Sing*.

Radio Times

New Mark Fenton Serial by David R. Dewar

Top tv news this week is that there will be a sequel to the record-breaking Saturday serial *The Broken Horseshoe*.

Entitled *Operation Diplomat* it will be written and produced by the famous radio partnership of Durbridge and Webster; Francis Durbridge of Paul Temple fame will write the scripts, and Martyn C. Webster will again be loaned from sound to produce.

"The new serial will start on October 23rd, and run for six weeks," I was told by Mr Webster. "The central figure will again be the surgeon hero of *The Broken Horseshoe* Mark Fenton, and the plot will deal with the search for a missing diplomat.

"But operation has another meaning, and that's how Mark Fenton becomes involved.

"We'll try again to carry the suspense and tension over from instalment to instalment. The real secret of a successful serial is to make people anxious to find out what happens next.

184

"There's nothing new about that – it's as old as the Pearl White thrillers of the old silent days. But it's vital. A serial must be quite different from a series."

The delight that most viewers will feel at this news will be tempered with disappointment because Mark Fenton will not, this time, be played by John Robinson, who created the character in *The Broken Horseshoe*.

Ironically, the fan mail and popularity this role brought him has been partly the cause of his being unable to sustain it in the sequel.

He became more sought after than ever by West End stage producers, and it is a commitment which prevents him from taking the Fenton role.

He has an important part in *Hanging Judge*, the Raymond Massey play at the New Theatre, and, by an apt coincidence, so has John Byron, a *Broken Horseshoe* team-mate.

In fact, the only member of the first cast who will remain in the successor will be Elizabeth Maude, daughter of Nancy Price, who has again been chosen as the sister.

And who is Mark the Second? – Scottish actor Hector Ross.

"I have given up a film part to play Fenton," he told me, "and I am sure it will be worthwhile."

Ross has been so busy on the legitimate boards (he made a big hit in *The Browning Version*) that it's some time since he appeared on tv, which he considers in many ways more exacting than screen or stage acting.

I learn that there is little likelihood of Paul Temple being transferred to tv. Francis Durbridge considers him a sound institution who should continue to be heard and not seen.

Glasgow Evening Times

Printed in Great Britain
by Amazon

35751297R00115